Hieronymus Bosch's triptych with the name "The Garden of Earthly Delights" depicts the so-called Tree Man, which is placed in the right 'Hell' panel.

Bosch's hell
"The suffering going on in this panel is not just on the physical level, it's also psychological: the souls are being driven mad by fear, anxiety, chaos and distress"
(*Jheronimus Bosch, Touched by the Devil* from Pieter van Huystee Film PRO on August 3, 2016).

The Tree Man is a fictional character who is a combination of humanity and a tree. He is afloat on fluid ground while looking back with a knowing smirk that is full of worldly wisdom. The look is not immortal, but earthly and thus fleeting as he views his own creation and offers a bubble of bliss that he, himself, can avoid for a time. Yet he can only provide it temporary lodging within to escape from the surrounding chaos and distress. But for how long can he stay afloat before the fall and eventual drowning of his protected community?
"We have bored a few holes through the door of the locked room; but somehow we do not seem to have discovered the key"
(Erwin Panofsky; *Early Netherlandish Painting, Its Origins and Character*. Cambridge: Harvard University Press, 1953).

Also by Sherry Marie Gallagher....

Felly van Vliet Mystery series

Murder On The Rocks!
(1st of the Felly van Vliet Mysteries)

Death By Chopstick
(2nd of the Felly van Vliet Mysteries)

The Poisoned Tree
(3rd of the Felly van Vliet Mysteries)

Other works

Boulder Blues

Dancing Spoons and Khachapuri

Uncommon Boundaries

Beyond Uncommon Boundaries

Sherry Marie Gallagher

Betrayal Of Bosch

A Felly van Vliet Mystery Series

Aisling Books
Mediator Media
The Netherlands

Aisling Books is a subsidiary of Mediator Media. Aislingbooks.com is registered with the *Stichting Internet Domeinregistratie* Nederland, Arnhem, The Netherlands.

For more information please contact:

MEDIATOR MEDIA
R. SCHUMANLAAN 73
4463 BD GOES
THE NETHERLANDS
E: info@mediatormedia.nl
W: www.mediatormedia.nl

Gallagher, Sherry Marie
Betrayal Of Bosch
© Sherry Marie Gallagher 2021

ISBN 978-1-329-23425-3
First Edition – 1st printing hardback
Cover designer: Rob Bitter

For

Patti, Lorraine and Dave

1

Femke McNeela's mother and father had been working remotely whenever they could until their little girl started her first year of compulsory school in the Netherlands. Under the Dutch system of paternal leave, they were able to be with her when she took those important first steps into toddlerhood. Now at five-years-old, the pre-schooler was ready for kindergarten, or the second group, as the Dutch refer to it, which left her parents little excuse not to return to the classroom and courthouse. Felly found herself enjoying working with students again, as research in cognitive semantics was interesting but left her all too often feeling isolated. Kieran too had longed for a more active role in the De Veer Law Group, and he got his wish when asked to become a junior partner. His long-held staff attorney position was one that he was more than happy to leave behind, which he texted as much to his wife while walking out the office door after the good news. In a celebratory mood, he saddled his bike and headed for the liquor store. While Kieran set out to restock their larder,

Felly texted family living in town to join them in an impromptu houseboat party.

The parents were first at the door. Martinus kissed his daughter on each cheek then once again for good measure, as her mother, Anneke, handed her a bouquet of autumn-coloured leaves and flowers. Felly admired the arrangement. 'Oh, how lovely. Did you get these at Happy Flower? All the colours match your outfit.'

The elder woman glimpsed her sweater and smiled. 'Yes, they do. I hadn't noticed. Congratulations, schat. Congratulations to you both. Kieran must be thrilled.'

'To bits,' she replied.

Anneke crossed over to the open bottles of wine atop the kitchenette countertop and poured herself a glass of red. Tinus helped himself to a shot of Dutch Jenever after setting down the covered dish in his hands. He took a sip of the gin, asking, 'Does this casserole need refrigeration?'

'Yes, of course it does,' said Anneke. 'It just needs reheating.'

Felly grinned at them both, eyeing her blonde, hazel-eyed mother in white slacks and yellow cashmere sweater. The woman had no problem speaking her mind, nor had she struggled to maintain the sporty figure she carried well into seniorhood. She glimpsed her father, thinking him handsome still. His vibrant eyes and chestnut hair had been passed on to her and her twin brother, Filip. 'What have you got there, Papa? Just put it in the fridge, yes, that is if you can find room.'

A rattle of bicycle chain locks was soon heard accompanied by a metallic clank of bikes set against the canal embankment railing. Then Filip and his Irish wife, Moira, burst through the sliding deck door. Wrapped around the brother's left wrist were strings of a half dozen helium balloons. 'Hello, everyone!' he said. 'We come bearing gifts.'

'Balloons!' squealed Femke. The child skipped in from the hall, her father following close behind. 'Look, Papa, balloons!'

'I see, I see.' Kieran smiled broadly. 'We were corralling cats into the back room, but I guess we can let them out. We just have to mind them from escaping outside.'

'Oh, them wee devils are sure to like these if they get a whiff of them.' Moira, handed him the airtight container she'd been holding.

'Salmon wraps?' He opened the box. 'They smell delicious.' Then he brushed aside fingerbowls filled with nuts and cheese and set the box on top of the kitchen counter. Lifting the lid, he took one out and bit into it. 'Mm, heavenly. And sure not to be wasted on the likes of them mischievous fluffballs. So, what's yer poison, Moira?'

'A Murphy's would be grand.'

He opened the fridge, grabbed a bottle, popped its lid on the counter and handed it to her.

She raised her beer to him. 'Sláinte.'

'Sláinte mhath, he said, raising his dram glass.' Their eyes met in unspoken recognition, almost tribal, then slid away to the sounds of a giggling child and her uncle. Filip had unfastened one of the helium balloons and inhaled some its contents. Now he was chasing Femke around the living room as he quacked like a duck.

Kieran manoeuvred his way around them to greet his father-in-law seated on the couch. Martinus rose, extending his hand with congratulations before telling him about the collection of artifacts he had seen that morning at the Egyptian exhibit in Leiden's National Museum of Antiquities.

9

Kieran had the elder man's ear while still managing to catch bits and pieces of his countrywoman's entertaining story told to their mother-in-law. Apparently, one of Moira's Irish aunts had phoned her that morning complaining about a a nanny goat and her kid sneaking into her kitchen. She had left the door ajar while cooling off a batch of freshly baked buns that were intended for an afternoon bridge club when the two goats sauntered in and consumed them all.

Moira laughed as she continued her story. 'I never before heard the auld woman in such a pickle. 'Jeannie Mac!' she cursed. 'And didn't those hoovering little shites gobble up the lot of 'em.''

Felly's mother dried her eyes, laughing with her. 'I imagine the bridge club left with goat cheese for a snack.'

'Oh, wouldn't Aunt Mary have liked that, now? So's, she told me that she made a mad skedaddle to the grocer and bought one of them Cadbury cakes.'

'Cadbury cakes?'

'They're delicious,' Felly told her mother. 'They taste just like the chocolates.'

'Oh? Then I'll have to try a slice someday then.'

'Remind me, and I'll bring you a box when we're back in Ireland.'

'Are you still planning on being there Christmas day? It's the Eve at our house, remember?'

'Don't worry, Ma. We haven't forgotten.'

She smiled at her daughter then rose from her chair, her eyes now locking onto her husband's. 'We should we be off, Tinus. 'We hadn't planned to stay long, just to pop in and congratulate Kieran.'

'Is it that time already?' The long, thin man glimpsed his Timex wristband.

'And, schat, whenever you feel like dinner, just pop the sauerkraut potato casserole in the microwave.'

Felly's eyes drifted over to the covered Pyrex bowl still sitting on the counter. 'I don't think we'll be eating much more tonight, not after all this booze and snacks. Kieran does love your casseroles, though. And neither of us will have to cook tomorrow. Thanks, Ma.' Then she called out, 'Poppie, your grandparents are leaving!'

'Again, well done, you,' Tinus said to Kieran. 'I know how you've been working long and hard for this promotion.'

Kieran smiled warmly. 'Yeah, I'm chuffed.'

'Bye Opa, bye Oma,' said the small face staring up at everyone with a yawn.

'Bye liefje,' said the grandparents. 'You're growing up so fast.'

'Bye Ma, bye Pa. Doei, dag.'

Kieran picked up his daughter, holding her in his arms as she waved at the departing elders. He set her back down, pyjama feet skipping along the bleached wood living room floor towards the balloons, their sagging streamers skating across the floor. He spied a half empty bottle of champagne and poured its contents into two empty glasses, handing one to his wife. 'My partnership fee will set us back some, but it won't take long to recoup the funds.'

'I'm not worried. You just landed that nice contract with the Bollenstreek.'

'Proost and sláinte to that. I believe they're one of the biggest flower-cutting companies in the Netherlands.'

'I believe you're right.'

They smiled and drank, their eyes following the few loose streamers floating out the lattice framed garden box kitchen window. They danced onto the waters of the Rijnkade, the tranquil river inlet where their houseboat was moored. And they floated across its surface, too light to sink.

The inlet was a result of mountain runoff waters beginning at the Franco-German border of the Swiss Alps and ending up forming the vast and picturesque river known as the Rhine. This passed through Germany and into the Netherlands while flowing into numerous tributaries and canals along the way. A few of these turned into still water ponds and ditches, but most meandered along until emptying into the North Sea. And one of the Rhine's many quays in North Holland's city of Leiden was the Rijnkade, where Felly and Kieran lived with Femke on a houseboat in a quiet neighbourhood tucked away from major traffic areas and perfect for raising a child. The canal of the Rijnkade was a slow moving one, and the waterfowl travelling its waters were spellbinding to watch as these swans, geese and ducks glided across the surface like skaters on clear ice.

Kieran shook off his daydreaming and rose to shut the window before the two mischievous Ragdolls noticed that it was open, though they were currently shimmying their backsides and tumbling over one of the balloons as Femke watched with glee.

Felly was so heartbroken when Nikki, her fat little Persian, had died. Afterwards, she decided not to raise any more cats. But Femke persisted and eventually got her way after proving she could manage an animal by the responsible manner in which she daily fed the goldfish she had won at the previous year's summer carnival. So, on her fifth birthday, two Ragdoll kittens had come home with Papa after work. This breed was of particular interest to Kieran, who would come home sharing a work colleague's stories about the family cat named Figaro who not only flopped when held, but he also fetched alongside Fleur, their fox terrier. And when Fleur required bathing, the Ragdoll stood close by and fearlessly lapped up water, as if somehow aiding the dog's plight. Figaro got along well with the children in the house too, Kieran's colleague told him. So, he did some further digging and found an online site that discussed the breed's origins. Felly grew more receptive, as well, when he pointed out to her that the breed was developed by a cross-breeding accident of a Persian/Angora mix with Burmese-like cats. All Felly had to hear was the word 'Persian', and she was sold.

After closing the window, Kieran went over to his daughter. 'Time for bed, poppie.'

'Can Pip and Puk sleep with me tonight?'

'Well, ye know how cats have minds of their own. But ye can try luring them under the covers with a catnip toy.'

'That's a great idea,' she said, her smile growing wider. 'Oh, kittens? Where are you?'

Moira entered from the aft deck just then. She and Felly's brother had married the year before when Taisce, the family farmhouse in Ireland, had been sold and its proceeds split among her and her cousins, Aidan and Sean, both still working for the Irish coastguard. She was pointing at the screen on her mobile phone when she came in. 'Did you see this, Fel?'

'What's that?'

'News about a Leiden professor drowning in 's-Hertogenbosch. That's in the province of Utrecht, right? Gads, that's just horrible.'

Felly read the screen with Kieran peering over her shoulder, reading it too.

'The article doesn't say much more than the woman's body was found drowned in a canal not far from

13

the train station. I should call and make sure our conference is still going.'

'Oh right,' said Kieran. 'Best to check on that.'

Her phone went off just then, giving her a start. 'Dr De Vos?' she said, speaking into it. 'No, I don't mind at all. Should I knock on the door? Oh, okay. Anything in particular I should be looking for? Right. No, no problem. See you then. Bye.' She raised a brow. 'That was Sebastian De Vos, the head of our anthropology section.'

'What did he want?' said Kieran.

'He asked if I'd mind swinging by the house of Dr Anneveldt. She's one of his staff.'

'Oh? Why does he want you to do that?'

She shrugged. 'Just checking on her, I guess. No bother, really. It's not out of my way.'

Kieran furrowed a dark blonde brow. 'So, why doesn't yer man go over there, himself?'

'I think he's at the hotel already, Kier. And I'm guessing Evi isn't. He's probably just checking on her is all.'

'I thought the conference begins on Saturday.'

She shrugged. 'Who knows what those anthropologists are up to. Maybe they had a team meeting a day earlier. I'm in the social sciences, which is a whole different section. We just happen to be under the same umbrella of humanities.'

Moira puzzled. 'So, why attend their conference then?'

'Because of this new information sharing programme our department head has us involved in. Anyway, Dr Huijsman asked if I'd join them, and as a personal favour I said, yes. Besides, I like Den Bosch, and I'm just thinking of it as a mini-vacation, all expenses paid. I just wish you were coming with me too, Kier.'

He gave her a warm smile. 'Maybe next time.'

'Jayzus,' said Moira, crossing herself. 'Do ye think it might have been this Evi woman who drowned?'

'Oh my God, Moira. Do you think?' Her eyes widening. 'I hope not. I hardly knew the woman, but still.'

Kieran reached for her hand. 'Just mind yerself while there, darlin'.'

'I'm all right. I know how to take care of myself.' She breathed in and out. 'So, do we still have a party going, or what?'

'I think I saw yer brother heading out to the deck,' Kieran said. 'I'll check and see if he needs a top up. Are ye sure you're alright, darlin'?'

'Fine and dandy.'

He smiled at his anglified Dutch wife and kissed her cheek. When he left, Felly glanced at the darkening window. 'Thanks again for picking up Femke from school tomorrow, Moira. If Kieran hadn't had that late deposition, he would've been able to do so.'

'Yer grand. I'll just have shepherd's pie ready, knowing that he'll be joining us for dinner too. It's a nice excuse to cook up a good Irish meal.'

'I thought shepherd's pie was English.'

'Ach no, it's been made in Ireland for ages. Me mam served it, and so did me Gran.'

'That reminds me.... I'd better put my mother's casserole in the freezer if you're cooking for them then. Kieran loves her cooking as much as he does yours.'

'What doesn't that man love to eat?'

'Speaking of which, please don't feed Femke too many home-baked cookies. She's had a few stomach bugs lately. I also don't want her getting too used to all those yummy things at your place. I always fear she'll never want to come home again to my bland cooking.'

'No worries,' Moira laughed, the dimple in her left cheek deepening. 'She couldn't part from them gremlin puff balls.'

'They are entertaining.'

One of the balloons popped just then and caught their attention as two fluffy white kittens raced across the hardwood floor, colliding with each other.

'Aw, jeez. Could they be any cuter? So's, let's go check on the lads and see what they're up to.'

'I can guarantee they're talking football.'

'I can't say much about yer Ajax, me being a diehard Cork fan and all.'

'Football is all the same to me.' Felly pointed to her empty glass. 'I could use a top up. You?'

'Another Murphy's would be grand. Any left?'

'I'm sure there are. It's Kieran's drink of choice, besides Paddy's Whiskey, that is.'

Moira grinned, nodding her head. 'Ye can take the boy from Ireland but ye can't take the Cork whiskey from the boy.'

'Ain't that the truth,' laughed Felly.'

2

Silver light streamed through the denim bedroom curtains as Felly awoke to the soft snoring beside her. In such a light Kieran looked the same to her as he had when he was one of the local guards in Youghal, Ireland. Youghal's notoriety came from its 11th century Viking settlements, which seafaring Scandinavians used as base camps to raid gold and silver from the monasteries along the southern coastline. In the 5th century, Declán of Ardmore had founded a monastery in the nearby county of Waterford and brought Christianity to the nearby provinces, as well as the whole of Ireland, even earlier than Saint Patrick. And the Irish Tourist Board designated this sleepy Irish town and seaside resort as an 'Irish Heritage Port', as its remains of rock-wall fortifications still displayed remnants of medieval architecture that whispered of its not so sleepy past. Today there are few traces left of the Viking plunderers, but an ancient carving of one of their infamous longboats can be spotted on a stone in St Mary's Collegiate Church.

When Kieran and Felly met, he had been recently promoted to inspector and was making his rounds to check up on a crime committed only days before Felly had come to teach a seminar. Their chance meeting had only happened because of her summer lodging, which was on a houseboat docked only metres away from where a teacher had been gruesomely murdered. So goes life and its fated connections.

When Felly was in graduate school, she came across the works of Plato on a reading list, his treatise on the predator/prey phenomena catching her interest. 'Who is the true victim?' he would ask his students. 'The predator or his prey?' According to the work, they would answer unanimously, 'His prey.' Then Plato would tell them, 'The prey, though wronged, can seek restitution and peace. Not so for the predator. He will carry his sins to the grave.' In the mythical dialogues, Felly read Plato's discourse on twin souls, thinking the notion presumptuously quaint and silly. Yet, when she and Kieran met, something had undeniably clicked. And theirs had grown into an unshakeable bond over the years.

Her husband turned to her just then. 'What is it, mo stór?'

'Only scattered thoughts, schatje. Go back to sleep.'

'Worries about the conference?'

'No, not really. I love you, Kieran.'

He touched her cheek and kissing her lips.

'Uh, thank you?'

'Is breá liom níos mó.'

'I think I'm in need of a translator?'

'No translation necessary. Actions speak louder.' He kissed her again, his kiss still lingering on her lips.

And she kissed him back, fire in her cheeks, just as tapping sounds were heard at the door accompanied by the scratching of tiny claws. They glanced at each other and sighed, knowing that their lovemaking would be put on hold. Kieran rose and slipped on pyjama bottoms before unlocking the door and greeting the child who burst into the room with two silky white and grey, black-nosed kittens. Felly took this as her cue to shower and dress while Femke bounced atop the king-sized bed. 'I'm queen of the hill!' she announced, giggling.

'And just who might ye be addressin'?'

The little girl shook her head, laughing. 'A big hairy monster!'

'Well, that may be. But I'm king of this mountain, and I don't give up without a fight.' He manned his pillowed post as child and cats toppled all over him.

'I'm the winner!' came a sudden small cry of victory.

'The definite article, alright.' He mussed her hair and picked up one of the cats, who'd just nipped his big toe and caused Femke to laugh out loud. 'Ouch, ye little devil. Okay, now time to get dressed. It's still a work and school day.'

'Awh,' the little girl pouted. 'Let's play hooky.'

'Not today, poppie. Now scoot.'

Late fall weather was setting in. After showering, Felly dressed in patterned Cashmere and black leggings. Her boots were lined with soft faux fur, and her woollen jacket and scarf would keep her warm enough for the short cycle to work. She turned to her daughter next and coaxed her into a puffy sleeved sweater dress. Then she braided her soft, fine hair into a side braid, which she fastened with candy-coloured hairclips. 'There, all done.'

'Mama, I don't like orange.'

'Your dress is browner than orange, and it looks smashing on you.'

'I don't wanna be smashed.'

'Go put on your blue one then, but hurry up. Papa's taking you to school today. Don't make him late for work.'

The little girl skipped into her room, singing in a fragmented mixture of the three languages she now spoke, one better or worse than the other depending on who she was with and where she was spending her time. Summers were spent mostly with family in Cork, and Gaelic was still spoken in the household.

Sinead and her husband, Mick, had taken over Kieran's place in Youghal, a generous gift to the youngest sibling and beau when they married. He had been glad to help out his little sister, and Felly was fond of her husband Mick. The two would drop in occasionally but mostly to check in on the health of their mother. Brigid insisted that she was in fine form and didn't need anyone to be checking in on her, though she enjoyed the attention and her children's company. Only one of Kieran's five siblings had never ventured far from the nest, but they saw more of Mairead's competition ribbons than they ever saw of her. His older middle sister did make an appearance on the occasion that she wasn't off on a training session or involved in shows. The more frequent lodgers, like the holidaying Kieran and Felly, had plenty of room in the McNeela home. The few stragglers showing up on a whim with overnight bags in hand would always have room made for them as well. And granddaughter Femke had slipped happily into this culture of her father's, a household of easy chaos and freely spoken Irish with its west country dialect. She'd be near native in her speech when returning home to the Netherlands, but she'd lose much of it again throughout the schoolyear. Moira would sometimes break into her native tongue with her around, though Kieran encouraged his daughter to converse with him in English. The international school Femke attended was also bilingual, though a second language wasn't mandatory in the younger groups where Dutch was primarily spoken, which was what she would mostly speak when her grandparents were around.

'I like this sweater, Mama.' Femke had returned wearing an embroidered sequined unicorn that flipped colours when stroked.

Felly winced then smiled her approval. 'Don't you look nice, poppie.'

'Mama, when are you coming back home?'

'I'm only gone the weekend. Papa will be joining you for dinner with Tante Moira and Oom Filip before bringing you back home.'

One of the hairclips got suddenly loose and fell to the floor, which Femke scooped up and deftly fastened back in her hair. 'Do we have to go to Opa and Oma's church Sunday? It's so boring. But if I put Pip and Puk in my backpack, they can play outside with me when that man in the white dress starts talking.'

'That's a clerical robe, silly.'

'Why does he talk so much?'

Stifling her laughter, 'Don't worry. We're not going to Opa and Oma's church on Sunday.'

'Papa is staying home with me, right?'

'Yes, he is. And Saturday he's taking you to see turtles in the Schildpaddencentrum. You'll like seeing all those turtles.'

'Can we get a turtle?'

'No, but they're fun to look at just the same.'

'Can I pick them up and pet them?' she said eagerly.

'I'm sure you can. Okay, so lunch is made and in your pack. Now I have to go finish packing, myself.'

21

Kieran poked his head around the corner just then, shaver in hand. 'Is my favourite girl raring to go?' He winked at Felly. 'My other favourite, I mean?'

'I was just telling Femke about the turtle centre you're taking her to on Saturday.'

'Right, that. I was telling a colleague yesterday and he said it's a bit disappointing.'

'Oh? How so?'

'The other patrons he and his son saw were mostly elderly folk in wheelchairs being pushed by their not much older companions. There weren't too many live turtles on display, either. And those that were he said were in sparsely decorated, high-walled glass tanks. Kids couldn't touch them, which was disappointing to his little lad. But they liked the displays of relics and African neckwear made from snake and turtle eggs. A favourite of theirs was some kind of wooden-looking instrument that he said was decorated with snakeskin and turtle platelets.'

Felly screwed up her face. 'That sounds grotesque.'

'His son even asked if it would make a hissing sound when played, like something from a Hogwarts' Smithereen snake.'

She laughed at that. 'Children have such imaginations, don't they?'

Kieran laughed with her. 'Then my colleague told his kid that it just might hiss at that, and he suddenly reached for it and got yelled at by the museum docent. Ha, poor kid. So, get yer coat on, poppie. Yer riding in back of my bike today.'

'Why can't I ride my own bike?'

'Because we won't be home till after dark is why.'

'Do you want some coffee, Kier? It's freshly made.'

He came into the kitchen and poured half a cup, slugging it down with a bite of toast. 'I'm sure you'll have a nice time in Den Bosch. It's such a great old city.'

'Honestly, I'd rather be here with you guys.'

'Be careful you're not turning into a house mouse.'

She laughed briefly, thinking that the Dutch expression had lost something in translation. 'I'll call you this evening when I'm settled in at the hotel, I promise.'

'Don't worry about us. We'll be grand.' He glanced at the wall mirror, shaking back loose strands of blond hair that were falling in his eyes. 'I need a haircut.' He looked back to his daughter. 'Ready? Give Mama a kiss before we head out the door.'

Cycling is an integral part of Dutch culture, and Femke would usually ride her bicycle to school alongside one or both parents. She sadly strolled over to her pink and white frame bike that was locked to the embankment railing. But her father shook his head, no. 'But I can ride in the dark.' She switched on the bike lamp. 'See, my bike has a light.'

'Nice try, but not this time, kiddo.'

'Child seats are for babies.'

'And big girls who want to go to the turtle zoo on Saturday.'

She poked out her lips. 'Okay, fine.'

Kieran clicked on the portable child seat that Felly's parents had brought over the day before. Bulky items such as the barely used car seat were hindrances in the precious little space available on a houseboat. Ankie and Tinus didn't mind storing a few things for their children either, which included Kieran's Bertone 2000. And their garage was spacious enough. The trade-off was that the parents could take the sports car out for a spin whenever they felt the yen to do so, which was seldom if ever.

Felly waved to the two people she loved more than this world before going back inside and collecting her coat and gloves. With bike cover removed and set aside, she stuffed the side saddlebag with her purse and strapped her carry-on luggage on the rack in back, securing it with elastic ties. The Ragdolls were crowded together and watching her from the kitchen sill, Pip stretching her paw as Puk chewed on a basil leaf in the herbal planter next to him. She grinned, waving to them and feeling ridiculous for doing so. They continued staring back as she cycled off toward the address that Sebastian De Vos had texted her.

It was a pretty stretch of green along the widening canal and row of redbrick houses. When she arrived at the Werfpark, she propped her bike against a small lattice fence across from it and rang the bell. She knocked at the door and waited, hearing nothing. She knocked again and peered through half-drawn venetian blinds of the large front window. No one was there. She texted this to De Vos and cycled on to school.

The linguistic aspect of Felly's social science curriculum looked at language-based materials, the everyday signs and symbols used throughout history. This included jargon, slang and art in all its forms. Other soft sciences shared the humanities department with her, but their studies differed in focus. The psychologists observed personal behaviours and psychoses; the sociologists, groups. And cultural anthropologists, such as Dr De Vos and his academic team, researched folk art, traditions and social habits. The man, himself, she knew only by a smile and handshake at interdepartmental meetings. So, why he had suddenly reached out to her was baffling, especially since she thought he could be off-putting with his old-school demeanour that to her came across as arrogant. Evi Anneveldt had been one of his head teachers, and the elder woman was popular with her students, though her mop of dishevelled hair and forever unlit cigarette at the corner of her mouth made Felly think more of a barfly at closing time than anyone's scholarly advisor. By contrast, Pascal van Houten, the department's younger and more progressive assistant professor, dressed himself in clean and classic fitted clothing. He too was popular, perhaps for different reasons than the eccentric elder, and she would often see him engaged in friendly conversation with one or two students clustered around his office door.

She walked through the department doors, hearing soft flute music coming from a corner office, the largest niche in the room. She caught sight of her mentor, Dr Ernie Huijsman, his recognisable shock of white hair muffled in headphones. His gaze was off in the distance, and she thought it best not to disturb him. Instead, she walked over to the cluttered desk of the department secretary, Jolanda Wiersma. Jolanda had attended Felly and Kieran's wedding along with the dean and his wife. Was it six years ago now? The secretary gave her a friendly smile but caught the strand of beads she was wearing around her neck on a desk handle when rising from her chair, her eyes now trailing after small plastic pieces bouncing across the linoleum floor. 'Jeetje, I'm the clumsiest person I know. Trudi makes these eyeglass beads. Kind of cute, aren't they? It's a hobby of hers. She says they help her concentrate, like a mantra. I hear her chanting 'ooohm' in her office sometimes when she's stringing them.'

Felly broke into a grin. 'Trudi, as in...?'

'Baas's secretary?'

Felly rested her purse and carry-on against the desk while pouring coffee from the office percolator. 'Oh, Dr De Vos's secretary. Langmeijer, is it?'

'That's her.'

'I really don't know their department well.'

'Then you must not have heard the news about Evi Anneveldt.'

'So, it was Professor Anneveldt who drowned? Oh my. De Vos had called and asked if I'd swing by her house on my way over. I did have my suspicions, especially when no one was home. Gosh, that's awful.'

'What an odd request of Baas. What did he hope you would see?'

She shrugged, sipping coffee. 'Like I said, I don't know their department, but it was on my way and I didn't mind doing it for him. Maybe it was just to put his mind at ease...or not. Dealing with someone dying can be such a painful process.'

'Yes, it can be. So, was everything in order?'

'I guess. Did she live alone? I didn't see signs of anyone else there.'

'Yes, she did. So sad. Maybe Baas was just hoping against hope.'

Jolanda inspected the small plastic bead she had stepped on just then as Felly bent down and picked up the few multicoloured shapes in front of her. She rolled them in her palm, handing them back to Jolanda. 'Were they close then, Baas and Evi?'

'Honestly, I'm not all that sure what goes on in that department. Theirs is a strange lot, and you didn't hear that from me.'

Felly winked and smiled. 'What was that?'

'And their conference? Nothing is deterring it from happening, especially after contracting the guest speaker.'

'Guest speaker even? Sounds intriguing.'

'Too bad you have the morning class. Most of your colleagues have already hooked up and are carpooling together. You could've ridden down with them.'

Felly eyed the wall clock. 'Speaking of which, I'd best be going.'

'Evi's drowning does cast a heavy shadow on things. Doesn't it?'

'It's very sad news, yes.'

'She has family in Den Bosch she was staying with when it happened.'

'She does? Why didn't De Vos know that? Oh well, whatever.' She sighed a brief sigh. 'How's Dr Ernie taking it?'

'Not good.' Jolanda motioned towards the dean's office. 'He's been sulking all morning. I'm just leaving him be for now, best thing.'

Felly looked over, still hearing music. 'Well, my class is about to start. Have a good weekend, Jolanda.'

'And you too at your conference.'

The midmorning class was a socio-linguistics course involved in a knowledge exchange programme coupled to an IT learning platform known as SPOC, where students were taught in small groups with added course material. This was evaluated through peer and faculty online reviews with a goal of developing higher levels of participation. So far, Felly was the lone staff member in her particular module, which she had set up for her students to apply the logical analysis skills they had been developing while examining cold cases. Bouncing their ideas off one another, they would analyse and argue collected data before running it through an internet programme which was designed to look for flaws or loopholes to challenge theories. Over the course of the semester, a few of these findings had even piqued the interests of agencies, such as the Dutch Department of Justice. This thrilled her and students alike after attempting to become a more interactive academic community, meaning working outside of the classroom. In this way, they took charge of their own learning while the professor team took on more of a coaching role, guiding them throughout. Felly also observed her motivated students linking into social discussion forums that were set up by the department. And their engagement grew dynamic, more so than with a traditionally styled learning module.

Felly wheeled her carry-on into a corner of the classroom and sat at a desk, where she rifled through folders she had taken out of her pack. 'Morning everyone,' she said. 'Today I want to talk about recreational communities.'

A young man with sandy blond pompadour gave her a sidewise smile. 'Do you mean actually creating something fun, even at the university level?'

She looked at him with sardonic amusement. 'Haven't you been enjoying all our stimulating cold cases?'

'Don't get me wrong. It's just that the word 'fun' and 'academics' don't mix.'

'And why not? Why not have fun, especially at higher levels of learning?'

'How about serious gaming as a learning forum?' said a student in faded jeans. 'What do you think, Professor? Couldn't that be given course credit?'

'You mean credit for using strategic gaming, Reinier?' the other replied. 'I don't know, like in DEFCON?'

Reinier scratched at a hole in his jeans. 'My little sister has an avatar in an online adventure program. It's an IT set-up that one of her middle school teachers has put together for his class. She's having some serious fun with that.'

Felly's interest piqued. The jeans scratcher was also in her academic writing class, and some of his 'out of the box' ideas were certainly engaging. 'Reinier, how do you believe this gaming....'

'Serious gaming,' he clarified.

'Okay, serious gaming. How does this encourage learning?'

'Simple. Everyone starts at a basic level and moves up. In my sister's science class, her teacher applies elementary forms of calculus to the steps they're taking. Seems pretty woke to me.'

'Maybe we could create something like an online *Whodunit!* as our last project?'

Felly stared into the brown eyes of the woman wearing an oversized lacy white sweater, whom she thought couldn't be much older than a secondary school senior. 'So, you're talking about a serious game that uses analysis to solve crimes? Interesting, Annemiek. Could we do that?'

The class grew excited, muttering to each other. 'Hell, yeah...I mean, heck yeah. What's to think about? Hmm...all the IT involved, for one. Putting it together for another.'

'Yes, it is a great idea, guys. But how would you go about building, or, should I say, programming, a storyline into this game? I honestly don't have a clue.'

Hands raised along with excited voices all talking at once. 'We do, Professor van Vliet! Yes, and those that don't can be shown by the others.'

'Okay, I'm listening.'

'First we get together and assess everyone's skillsets.' Annemiek smoothed the patterns in her dark leggings with her darkly painted nails. Then she went on. 'I know that Lucas and I are good at storytelling.' She motioned to the tall thin student who had spoken earlier, his pompadour bobbing as he smiled at her.

Then Reiner took the floor. 'Minke and I could handle coding.'

A young woman in a pinstripe jacket agreed with him. 'I'm good at design, yes.'

Felly eyed her keenly. 'And then what?'

'Like Annemiek says,' spoke Lucas. 'We can design a storyboard. Easy peasy.'

'And asking key questions as we divide them into sections of topics.' Annemiek ticked them off, saying: 'The telling, the planning, the content.'

'What does that mean, exactly? Explain it to me,' said Felly.

'Meaning to ask questions, like what's our narrative?'

'And should the game include a narrator? Hey, like Detective Van der Valk,' said Lucas, grinning.

Annemiek grinned back. 'You mean the Dutch detective who was really British?'

'That's the one. Great series.'

'If we're using Van Der Valk,' said Reinier, 'we should have the setting be Amsterdam. That's where he was based, anyway.'

'Well, it doesn't have to be him.' Felly was grinning along with her fired-up students. 'Most importantly you need to think about motives and outcomes.'

'We could also think about set-up, building a setting, movements,' said Minke.'

'Yeah, and the game's logistics.'

Minke nodded her head at Reinier. 'Like is it going to be in levels, you mean?'

'Exactly, along with thoughts on how all this progress is going to be saved. We should be able to check ourselves individually, as well as in a group...that sort of thing.'

Annemiek asked, 'This could be our capstone project, right?'

Felly scanned the room, seeing the show of hands that agreed. Only one in the room seemed hesitant, and Felly made a note to talk to Lotte Wehkamp after class. 'First I'd like to see some kind of paper storyboard that includes a rough timeline and task list. In other words, everyone needs to be somehow involved. You can show me next week, though. Meanwhile, we can chat online if you run into any snags. Just not this weekend because of the teachers' conference.'

Heads nodded as students began pulling out their phones as they packed up and shuffled out of the room, a few excitedly chatting about the project.

'Lotte?' She went over to the student who had lingered behind with whisps of flaxen hair almost covering her eyes. 'Why didn't you raise your hand? Don't you like the project?'

'It's not that,' she said almost in a whisper. 'I'm just not technically savvy enough to contribute much. And if this our capstone project, I'm worried about my final course grade.'

31

'You've been one of our strongest project analysers all term. I don't think you need to worry.'

'I do if I can't contribute.' She brushed loose strands of hair from her face. 'I'm majoring in neuro-linguistics. Analysis is something that comes natural to me, but I don't know anything about gaming...online or otherwise.'

'The way your classmates are describing it, I think you'll find your niche easily enough and fit right in.'

'Oh? In what way?'

'Well, the team that's designing the narrative will need to think about how to apply strategies towards specific outcomes. That's right up your alley. Yes?'

She nodded, brightening. 'Yes, it is. And I don't have to do any programming?'

'Just stick with the creative students and leave the coding to the designers.'

'Okay, I guess I can do that. Thanks, Professor.'

'Not at all.' They left the room together then parted ways, Lotte to her next class and Felly to the station to catch a train to Den Bosch.

3

Den Bosch, formally 's-Hertogenbosch, is loosely translated as the 'the Duke's forest', which was an original landholding developed into a fortress to secure a Duchy, which was the inherited property of Duke Henry. Over time this fortress grew into what's now the capital city of North Brabant in the southeast of the Netherlands. The charm of this old city was not lost on Felly, but her interests lay in the works of one of its native sons, the famous visionary painter Jheronimus Bosch. Bosch was born into a family of German Catholic artists who had moved to Holland in the late 15th century and lived in the province of Brabant throughout the 16th. Little is known of Bosch's early life and how it might have influenced his later work that played on the moral failings of humanity in a whimsical way. Felly saw his creations as semantical feasts of thought and feeling. She felt that one could study his fantastical illustrations for years and still argue the depth of their meaning. And behind it all was a shared belief by many that he was poking fun at some of our more basic human failings.

After leaving the train and station, Felly entered a square and crossed the busy street beyond as she listened to the sounds of her carry-on clattering down the city's cobbled streets like horses' hooves strolling into town. First, she stopped at the popular Jan de Groot Banketbakkerij and slid into a booth, ordering a dark chocolate éclair that the locals called 'Bossche Bollen' for its round pastry puff shape. She ate only half, because the cream filling was too rich for her. She left the rest on the plate and continued on to the square, staring in wonder at the 12th century architecture of some of the remaining older stone houses that displayed ornately gabled façades. The gambrel roofs were of a colonial design, their curved eaves running along the buildings.

The Golden Tulip Hotel on the market square was where Felly was staying with her university colleagues. This building hadn't always been a hotel but was once the town post office. Later it was turned into a restaurant. And now a hotel, which was refurbished and extended as clientele grew over the years with the owners doing their best to keep up with the times while retaining the building's old-world charm. There were revolving doors at the entrance which led into the lobby's front desk. As she entered and checked in, she discovered from the desk clerk that she would be share a room with Trudi Langmeijer, Dr De Vos's secretary. The cheapness of her department's double-booking took her somewhat aback. She thought it best not to complain but just enjoy the free accommodations and services.

It was still early enough to explore the town, so Felly left her carry-on at the front desk and headed in the direction of an art centre dedicated to the painter, Jheronimus Bosch. Many of his reproductions were now on display, which included an original astronomical clock he had constructed. This doomsday clock depicted the Last Judgement in the artist's imaginings and was the centrepiece of Saint John's Cathedral throughout the 16th century. Its sole purpose, other than telling time, was to keep the local parishioners in line as they lived out their lives in fear of wrongdoing. Bosch's creations had the effect of juxtaposing the nightmarish with the humorous, which is why in modern times his imagery is to this day so provocative. Felly's personal favourite was the triptych of panels in oil, named 'The Garden of Earthly Delights'.

As she set out to find the art centre, Felly was well aware that she would be only viewing the reproductions of oil paintings that were now scattered across the globe: some in the Americas, others in Europe and a smattering found in New Zealand and Australia. The large Spanish collection was due in part to a 16th century Catholic king who had scouts buying up the misunderstood painter's work forty years after his death. Yet, King Phillip II had also failed to grasp Bosch's intentions, using what he misunderstood to be the meaning of the imagery to justify personal bigotry that led to the expulsion of a large Muslim population from Spain during his reign.

Using works of art to justify violence had formed a part of the armoury of art as propaganda, which was one of the chosen weapons of the Counter-Reformation. Bosch was merely a painter of a medieval period in human history that was verging on a new age of renaissance. Many of his works have since been analysed as phantasmal, even verging on drug-induced surrealism. But nothing of the painter and his personal life was revolutionary, except that his work was strikingly imaginative while dealing with biblical themes of 'good and evil' that he, himself, believed in. The highly creative tryptich of Bosch's 'Garden of Lusts', which has been loosely translated as 'The Garden of Earthly Delights', can be stared at for hours with many personal takes and social suppositions. The first tryptich of oil on an oak panel is a scene before the biblical fall, a perfected vision of humanity's naive forefathers, Adam and Eve. The second tryptich morphs into the passing of time, where perhaps the children of God's fallen perfection are shown acting out their sensory pleasures as they throw caution to the wind while hedonistically experiencing life to the fullest. The third tryptich displays the fall, Bosch's version of hell in the supposed afterlife where human beings were tortured by the very lusts that had consumed them as they lived.

Felly spent some time examining each panel, the characters, in her mind, looking to be having more of a frolicking good time than involving themselves in anything lascivious. Her five-year-old, she knew, would especially like the luscious strawberry designs. Her personal favourite was the 'tree man', his torso exposed from behind like a cracked egg supporting a community in miniature that went about its business oblivious to the world outside its parameters. The tree man's face looked suspiciously like the face of the painter. And there was speculation that the mirrored image was having a private laugh while looking back on his own creation. Bosch's vision of the 'devil in the detail', thought Felly, was one musing over the fine line between humanity's gusto and its fragile nature. She thought a good question for the piece might be if freewill would evolve or devolve a society.

Glimpsing the time on her phone screen, she thought she could squeeze in one more exhibit before closing time. The Museum of Design had sparked another interest because of its recent publicity over its director's controversial decision to display a documentary of the works of Arno Breker, and a few others of his era. This display was done on the 75th anniversary of the liberation of Den Bosch from Nazi occupation during the Second World War. And, after suffering through heated protests and bad media press, he stuck with the decision to continue showing hanging swastikas and other symbols from the Nazi era. These, the director claimed, were powerful reminders of the horrors of a darker time in Europe's recent past. How easily they had been manipulated to create the hell that followed. In his statement, he pointed out euphemised examples of such acts as ethnic cleansing that was committed under the guise of 'lebensraum', meaning 'more living space for a country's citizens'. Thankfully, Hitler had failed in his desire to make Germany great again, at least not in the way he had envisioned it.

The director had also stipulated that photo taking was expressly forbidden during the exhibition, as he didn't want his intentions either misunderstood or misrepresented. Felly thought this understandable but also a great pity that she couldn't show Kieran how strikingly brash and cruel some of these images truly were. He would just have to later come see for himself.

On her way out the door, Felly checked her Trip Advisor, looking for reviews about an Indonesian restaurant mentioned by one of her students. Reinier Nolten told her that his family lived in Den Bosch, which was still home to him when he was not in school. The place was a local hangout, he said. And a map search showed it to be just a fifteen-minute walk from the museum.

She found the corner building easily enough and entered through a corridor of tinkling bells. 'Are you still serving lunch?' she called in.

A dark-skinned couple glimpsed her from behind the bar in back, which really did look to Felly like a local meeting spot, especially with the elderly lady perched atop a middle barstool with tea in hand and shopping bag underfoot.

'Come in, come in," said the man dressed in white jeans and black shirt. "We're just beginning our dinner menu."

'Am I too late for lunch then? Or can I order à la carte?'

'Yes, of course. À la carte is possible.'

The large room with clusters of wooden tables was filled with natural light that streamed through huge angular windows, making everything glow warmly. The man pulled out one of the embroidered cushion chairs. 'Please sit,' he said.

She skimmed the menu, and everything looked delicious, so delicious that she wished she were staying for dinner. 'I'll have a pot of jasmine tea. And...is Gado Gado possible to order à la carte?'

'Yes, of course. And steamed coconut rice, perhaps?'

'A small bowl, please. That would be nice.'

The teapot came with a basket of kroepoek, which were deep fried crackers made with tapioca starch and minced prawns salted in garlic. 'We make these fresh, ourselves,' the man told her. She bit into one as he stood over her, smiling. 'Very tasty, yes?' Then he poured her tea. 'Are you here visiting our city today?'

'I'm mixing business with pleasure,' she said, taking another chip. 'This is so good. I haven't been in Den Bosch since I was a child. A pity, yes?'

'Where are you from?'

'Leiden, and one of my students recommended your place.'

'Oh, that's nice.'

'Den Bosch isn't such a big city. Perhaps you know Reinier. Nolten's the surname. He grew up here.'

'Why, yes. My wife and I know the Nolten family well. We go to church with them.'

'Church?' Somehow her grunge looking student with holes in his jeans didn't fit the picture.

He looked back to the bar. 'Candra? This woman is Rein's university teacher from Leiden.' The woman behind the bar smiled up at her then continued chatting with the local.

'It was nice of him to recommend our restaurant to you. You can too. It'd be much appreciated. You like Indonesian food, yes?'

'I love it. I'll come back again with my husband and daughter. We'll have a proper meal then, perhaps a rice table?'

'You do that. That would be nice. And I'll be right back with yours.' The man returned with a plateful of steamed vegetables, fried tofu, small chunks of potatoes and egg covered in peanut sauce. Included with the meal was a white porcelain bowl of steaming rice sprinkled with fried coconut flakes.

She inhaled the pleasant aroma. 'Lekker! It looks so tasty.'

'Enjoy your meal. And give our regards to Rein when you see him next. We miss him at church.'

Her eyes drifted to the indifferent women in back. 'Thank you, I will,' she said, all smiles.

The return to the town square was not an uncomfortable walk, though done more slower than before with a full load of rice in her belly. She now wished that the charming venue had been more like many of the modern Van Der Valk hotels where she could go for an evening swim to work off all the calories she had consumed that day.

Upon entering the lobby, Felly caught sight of her colleagues. They flagged her over, drinks in hand. A staff person was bringing refills and followed her to the lounge area, taking her order. 'Did you just arrive?' said the sandy-haired assistant professor. 'We're on our second round. You need to catch up.'

'I checked in earlier but have been out exploring the city,' she said.

'Oh, that's sounds nice. Sorry you missed out on the carpool, though. Did you go by train?'

'Yes, I had a morning class. So, it wouldn't have worked out, anyway.'

'And where did you go exploring? Did you take in the Bosch museum?'

'That and the one of design.'

'Ah, the Breker exhibit.' Pascal rubbed the close-cropped stubble around his jawline. 'Quite the controversy.'

'It was thought-provoking, I'd say.'

'Did you take any photos?'

She shook her head, no. 'They weren't allowed.'

'Really? That's odd. I wonder why not?'

'Well, you could vlog them, for one thing.'

'And what's the harm in that?'

'I guess it would depend on your mindset.'

'The media was all over it, that's for sure.'

'You younger generations haven't been affected by the traumas of parents who'd experienced the occupation first-hand,' commented Dr De Vos. 'My parents are no longer living, but the few stories they told us kids were hair-raising. The rest they refused to speak of, not to their dying day.'

'I'm glad those days are over, Dr De Vos,' said Felly, eyeing him with kindness.

'Please, call me Sebastian. We're off the clock here. Ah, but there's still so much unrest in the world. Who can really say that this hateful chapter of man's inhumanity to man is long over?'

She studied the faces of her department colleagues, wondering if she dared bring up the topic of Evi Anneveldt and her drowning before deciding against it. 'So, I'm looking forward to tomorrow. All this talk about creating interactive communities has certainly got my students excited.'

'Oh? How so?' De Vos was seated beside Felly's weekend roomy, his secretary Trudi Langmeijer. She also noticed both their eyes were red.

'Well, my students are developing an online *Whodunit!*' she said. 'And they're plugging critical thinking strategies into the game they create, which will help them solve the crimes.'

'Intriguing. Sounds like they'll need some programming skills, though.'

'I know,' she said. 'They tell me they're up for the challenge, though. Serious gaming they're calling it.'

'It's brave of you to take that on, very brave.' He tossed down what looked like Jenever, the Dutch whiskey Felly's father liked to drink.

'I'm going to let them attempt it, anyway.'

'Will they have individual avatars marking their interactions?' asked Pascal.

'I'm not sure yet how I'm going to monitor it all.'

'I wouldn't mind assisting.' There was an unmistakable gleam in his eye. 'That is, if you wouldn't find my help an intrusion.'

'Not at all. You'd certainly be welcome. I don't want to discourage my students, but I don't know a thing about the art of gaming.'

'It's simple once you get the hang of it. Even a child can do it. And does, obviously. Take Minecraft or Roblox as examples.'

Felly thought of her own five-year-old's love of these child games. If Femke could create virtual Lego-like worlds on her iPad with changing skins and portals then she certainly could get a handle on her students' *Whodunit!* project. 'So....' She scanned the faces of everyone, now daring to bring up the subject on her mind. 'What happened to Evi Anneveldt? Any news?'

Dr De Vos blinked and cleared his throat. 'We don't know what happened. The police haven't been very forthcoming.'

'I was in the office earlier today,' said Felly. 'The dean, for one, is taking it badly.'

'As are we all.'

'Yes, I can imagine. I confess I didn't know her well at all. Jolanda tells me she'd been staying with family here? Has anyone been talking to her relations?'

He met her gaze with a rush of colour. 'We'll know soon enough, Felly.'

'I'll leave it at that then. It's been a long day.'

'Yes, it has,' he agreed.

'Speaking of which,' piped in Trudi, 'it's getting late and we have a full agenda planned for tomorrow. Breakfast first, of course, and....' She took off her glasses, Felly noting the beaded eyeglass chain that dropped to her chest as she searched through a designer bag made from Coach's "signature C" jacquard material. 'Here's our schedule, and everyone's participation is expected,' she said briskly as she handed out copies. 'Please do your best to follow our tight schedule.'

This was also a cue to rise and exchange pleasantries before heading off to the designated hotel rooms. Felly lingered to check her phone messages, returning one immediately. 'Hello, poppie. Why aren't you in bed?'

'Papa said I could stay up to say goodnight,' replied the sleepy child's voice.

'Did you have lots of fun today?'

'I did, Mama, but Tante Moira says silly things sometimes.'

'Oh? Like what?'

'She said she was drinking her cat. And I said you don't drink cats! And she said, no muppet, me gat, me Guinness.'

Felly grinned. 'Love you, little one. Sleep well.'

'Night, Mama. Papa wants to say sumpthing.'

'Hi Papa, are you drinking your gat now too?'

He laughed. 'I wish I were.' His voice was warm and comforting to her. 'How's Den Bosch?'

'Nice, but it would be better shared with you and Femmie. The conference hasn't actually started yet, but I did to take in some sightseeing.'

'Oh? How was that then?'

'I visited the Jheronimus Bosch art centre, which was interesting but noticed that none of his originals were there.'

'That's too bad. Where'd they all go?'

'All over the world. A few in Rotterdam, others in Ghent. My favourite, 'The Garden of Earthly Delights', is in Madrid. The reproductions were nicely done, I thought. And the astronomical clock's an original. It was fun to see, but a bit of a laugh.'

'Why the laugh?'

'It's hard to envision all those medieval countryfolk being spooked by what looked to me like naked Barbie dolls wired up to leap through a painted plywood inferno.'

Kieran chuckled. 'I wouldn't mind catching a glimpse of that, myself.'

She went on. 'Then there was this lone figure wired to pass through heavenly plywood gates. Truly a waste of living, all this heaven and hell business, if you ask me.' He was still laughing as she continued. 'Oh, and I visited the design museum. You know the one that's been in the news recently?'

'And is that something worth seeing?'

'I found it frankly disturbing, more in what the imagery represented than in the works themselves.'

'Hmm, well, I wouldn't mind checking that out too. Here at home, we had a lovely dinner with Moira and yer brother. Femke takes to them so.'

'Did she bake her shepherd's pie? I had Indonesian, myself.'

'Tasty, was it? No, we had Irish stew and homemade soda bread.'

'What a treat. Gosh I'm tired. We're full-on tomorrow, and then I should hopefully be back late Sunday afternoon.'

'Miss ye, mo stór.'

'I miss you more. And have fun at the turtle centre tomorrow. Just don't bring any turtles home with you.'

'We won't.'

'No matter how much Femke begs.'

'I swear on me father's grave, we won't.'

'Okay then. Bye now.

'Bye love.'

She slid her phone into her bag, yawning as she headed for the lift. She was good and tired. Good, she thought. She would be tired enough not to notice her roomie there either. But when she slipped quietly into the room, Trudi Langmeijer was nowhere in sight.

4

Felly awoke the next morning, lingering in bed before rising to plug in a small water cooker in a snack corner with mini-fridge underneath. She poured a complimentary coffee packet into a cup, adding boiling water and taking a sip before putting in sugar and cream to soften the taste. She took a leisurely shower in the ensuite bathroom, towel-dried her hair and flipped on the television while scrolling the remote in search of a local news station. The drowning would have been a shock to the small Brabant farming community and tourist town, its residents hearing mostly about petty crimes of vandalism such as a stolen bicycle here or there, a reported shoplifting, or a kerfuffle at the local coffeeshop that sold marijuana to smoke on the premises, which sometimes resulted in small-time drug trafficking arrests. Nothing much more than this.

She stumbled upon a morning news broadcast, waiting patiently while hearing about lost cattle recoveries, housing prices, a dip in market sales...then, at last, a local restaurant maintenance man being interviewed about the drowning. She sat on the bed, suddenly all ears.

Apparently, he'd been closing up the Bolwerk Brassiere, a restaurant along the city's Dommel canal. He'd been checking the electrics, as some lights had shorted out during a twenty-one-year old's birthday bash. And he had heard the loud splash as he was checking the fuse box. There was no fowl or fish in the water that could have made such a sound, he had told the reporter. So, he went out on the terrace to investigate. The cleaning team were long gone. It was only him remaining, and he couldn't see over the waters for the lack of moonlight. He hadn't known what else to do except to report it. As the man spoke, Felly remembered how she had walked past that very brassiere that afternoon, which was not far from the railway station. The modern two-tiered building's design reminded her of the hulk of a ship, its concrete roof just above street level and fashioned into a balcony with scenic overlook of the river canal below. She had paused even, thinking its design unusual, the way it jutted up against the canal. One could only access it either by taking a lift down to the restaurant or walking the stone steps to the terrace on the water's edge.

No further information was given after the interview except for a brief statement by the police. Basically, they hadn't discovered anything untoward upon arriving at the scene and taking the statement of the concierge. It had been the following morning when two boys on a dinghy fishing for minnow had butted their boat against the body. The later identified woman had been tangled up in foliage alongside a huge weeping willow by the bridge named after the old Dutch Queen Wilhelmina. Felly caught her breath when the broadcast station's camera panned across the canal bank and focused briefly on a sandwich board with Jheronimus Bosch's 'Garden of Earthly Delights'. The tree man looked sinister in this replica, as if he were gloating at anyone gazing on his image. It was then she noticed the time and quickly threw on her clothes before leaving to join the others at the morning's seminar.

The Jeroen Bosch Zaal wasn't the biggest conference room in the hotel but large enough to hold a long table and chairs, as well as a counter that now sat snugly against a far wall and was set up with a Krug® coffee machine and snacks. When she walked into the room, Felly's colleagues were still clustered around the coffee bar chatting leisurely. She greeted them there as she pressed the machine to manufacture a quick latte.

'So, are you braced for today's lecture?' said the department's young assistant professor. 'I hear it's going to be about innovative learning trends.'

'Hm, so I've heard. Focusing on what in particular? Do you know?'

'Everything under the sun, apparently.'

'I thought the expression was nothing new under the sun.'

'Oh right. Well, then nothing and everything,' he said with a snicker.

'Sounds like a Hemingway quote to me. Have you read 'The Sun Also Rises'? It's a masterpiece in literature.'

'No, I haven't. Is it something you'd recommend?'

'That depends on if you're into disillusioned expats wandering around 1920s Europe while looking for thrills and chills to rid them of their wearisome post-war blues.'

He laughed. 'Sounds like my life's story.'

She grinned back. 'Hemingway may have been a genius, but I still think he's an acquired taste.'

'Speaking of thrills and chills, what about this new project you've got your socio-linguistics class engaged in?'

'You mean our serious gaming project?'

Pascal nodded his head. 'Some of my students can't stop talking about it.'

'That is so nice to hear. I'm admittedly out of my depth with IT gaming, though. I haven't a clue how to begin, let alone how I'll be monitoring everything as it progresses. I'm planning on figuring it all out as I go.'

'A risk taker, are you?'

'Either that or a fool.'

'Just get progress reports along the way. I'm sure students will cooperate with that.'

'I'm sure they will. They seem so keen and their energy is infectious.'

'There you go. Nothing to worry about.'

'But those who are more tech savvy may have the edge on the other, even brighter, students. I'm worried that they might stumble over the technology aspect of it.'

'I think you'll be surprised how second nature it is to this generation. Remember they're being raised from cradle to grave with all this stuff.'

She finished her coffee and threw the empty cup in the bin. 'I just need to think about how best to promote the skills of those better at things like storyboarding and organising. I reckon they'll need a task list too, to account for who all is doing what.'

'As far as programming goes, you have a few of my first-year seminar course students, like Reinier Nolten, who are certainly up to the task.'

'Reinier is actually the one who came up with the serious gaming idea.'

'Yes, he's brilliant. Another creative student that we're losing to finance.'

'Is gaming big business?'

'It can be, yes. You have to keep abreast of the ever-changing cloud of technology.'

'I would imagine so, but it's definitely not my field. I like sticking to what I can see. Or at least what I can make sense of in the real world, which to me is mindboggling enough.'

He grinned. 'There are those who'll always feel a bit lost in these times.'

'I'm a modern dinosaur, myself,' she admitted.

'Come now, surely not. I'm still in my twenties. Well, just barely. You?'

'Thirty-something, yes.'

Brows slightly raised. 'I wouldn't have guessed. Age is such a relative concept, isn't it? Just like time.'

They do go together,' she smirked.

'But surely your IT savvy students could be a system of support by proxy.'

'Of course, which is also why monitoring is going to be important...just to ensure a team effort. I don't want the project to turn into something like 'The Apprentice', that nasty TV series that aired awhile back.'

'Oh yeah, that was noxious. I never understood the hype.

'I think classmates should be feeling free to tap into their own skill bases. In that way they can explore what they have to offer without feeling pressured or threatened. I liken it to a bottom-up, not top-down, capstone project.'

'Exploring what they have 'under the knee', as we say?'

'Exactly.' Felly mulled over the amusing Dutch expression that meant to tap into one's own resources, which was yet another example of something losing its meaning in translation.

Dr De Vos addressed the room just then, his reading glasses perched on the end of his nose. 'Has everyone got a coffee? Good. Take a seat, and I'd like to welcome Professor Jens Borsen, who has come here from Copenhagen's Institute of Innovative Media. This morning he will be discussing narratives in online learning strategies.'

Pascal shot Felly a brief smile as he took the chair next to hers. All eyes were now trained on the balding Dane who greeted everyone, then proceeded to weave his words in cadence to the rhythm and flow of flashing images lighting up the pull-down wall screen. All eyes but Felly's. She was lost in thought, the circumstances of Evi Anneveldt's death plaguing her. A happenstance, everyone had called it, an unfortunate accident. But to her there were so many unanswered questions. For one, what had the woman been doing at the canal in the middle of the night? Was she meeting someone there? Felly scanned the gathering of colleagues who were calmly engaged in the guest speaker's rhetoric. Their short-lived grieving seemed so callous to her. She felt something was off. And it all had happened only a kilometre's distance from the hotel. She shuddered involuntarily.

'Cold?' whispered Pascal. 'We could get the heat turned up for you.'

'I'm fine, Pascal, but thank you.'

Happenstance was what Felly's husband Kieran had called their first encounter. She was on a rented houseboat along the quay and Kieran, the local investigator, had been asking a few questions before realising that she hadn't been there long and was not a witness. He stayed for the offered cup of tea, anyway, encouraged by her boiling kettle. She had liked the way he said 'ye' when speaking to her, which was a part of the local dialect. There was an added dilation in the pupils of his eyes, which made her blush. And he later confessed how he liked her on the spot. She wished he were there now, watching, observing her colleagues with her.

Felly had come to believe not much had occurred in life by happenstance. Rather, the paths she had known and followed had been, for the most part, purposely thought out and carried through. Granted, the coincidences surrounding the meeting of her life partner had been unusual to her, but she had encouraged the flirtation as well. As for the fate of murders that seemed to surround her, she felt that these could have all been preventable. Most, she observed, had occurred out of fear and misunderstanding. The taking of life in China was greed-based, that and the personal embarrassment that followed a business deal gone south. These had nothing to do with chance, but rather intent.

The incident affecting her most had occurred with the mishaps of a childhood friend, her sorely missed colleague, Thijs Brugman. Thijs had been victim to attempted murder, leaving him scarred more by a broken heart than anything physical. These days, however, her old friend and colleague appeared to be doing fine. When they last face-timed, Thijs swore to her that all was well and good with his new life as a New York City casting agent.

She breathed in and out then returned her attentions to the man wrapping up his presentation. Blah blah blah, and a round of gentle applause. Instructions to pair up were now followed, and she saw Dr De Vos smiling at her.

'Een stuiver voor je gedachten?' he said. 'But can thoughts be given away so cheaply as with a penny?'

Her eyes darted round the room for Pascal, locking on him standing over the coffee apparatus chatting up the hotel clerk who was emptying out little cups of ground flavoured beans.

'You're stuck with me for your partner, I'm afraid.'

She turned back to the man. 'Sorry, my mind is elsewhere. What are we pairing up for again?'

'Our speaker would like us to share personal narratives.'

'Oh?'

'Yes, he wants us to share something about who we are and where we're going.'

'Well, you know who I am, and I can't stop thinking about Evi Anneveldt.'

'Tragic news.'

'It was never clear to me exactly why you called and asked if I'd check on her house, especially after Jolanda told me yesterday morning that Evi had been staying with relatives here in Den Bosh. Surely you knew that too.'

His face fell. 'Yes, you got me there. Sometimes people in shock do stupidly pointless things. I don't know what I was hoping for, really. It's been a nightmare.'

She took his hand and gently squeezed. 'My apologies for seeming insensitive.'

'Not at all. It was a valid question.'

'Have you heard anything more since we last spoke?'

He sighed. 'Sadly no. Have you?'

'No, nothing at all.'

'Evi was on compassionate leave, you know.'

'I didn't know that, Dr De Vos.'

'Please, Felly. Drop the formality and call me Baas. And, yes, it was a personal matter.'

'I see. Well, Dr... uh, Bass?'

He raised a greying brow. 'Yes?'

54

'So, I'm a linguist and I'm about to go to lunch.'

'What's that?'

'You wanted to know who I am and where I'm going?'

The gloom lifted and he laughed. 'Touché, shall we go then?' He turned from her as she nodded her head. 'Time to wrap this up, everyone. We're now heading over to the room set up for lunch. Great talk, Jens.'

The Dane returned the smile, and the two men walked out together with the others trailing behind.

The session scheduled after the noon break was to end in the sharing of personal narratives to demonstrate how, according to the visiting host, such an exercise could benefit students with their academic and career planning. Before they could begin, however, they were interrupted by two uniformed police officers from the local station in Den Bosch, the woman speaking first. 'We apologise for the intrusion, but we're here to ask a few questions. Sir?' She turned to the cultural anthropology head. 'Are you Dr Sebastian De Vos?'

He nodded warily.

'And you have a woman who's been in the employ of your department, a Dr Eveline Anneveldt?'

'Surely anything you want to know about our deceased colleague can be best done in a call to the department secretary.'

'Pardon, sir, but this is a possible homicide and we want to cover all the bases. First we'd like to know the time each of you arrived at the hotel.'

Pascal piped in. 'An easy answer. We all carpooled together.'

Felly gingerly flashed a finger. 'Except for me.'

'Oh? And when did you come, miss?'

'That's missus, she corrected. 'I arrived yesterday afternoon by train...after a morning class I taught in Leiden.'

The officer turned back to De Vos. 'None of you have been here before then?'

De Vos shifted his gaze to his secretary, Trudi Langmeijer. Then he said, 'Of course, we've all been before. Den Bosch is not that far away. What is it? About 120 kilometres from Leiden?'

Trudi fiddled with her eyeglass chain, rubbing the beads. 'Give or take, yes.'

'Officer Bram and I have come from the family home where the deceased's parents told us about her plans to attend this conference. She was going to attend, yes?'

Felly glimpsed De Vos, noting his irritation. 'She was expected, of course, but since she'd been with family, we'd given her some leeway.' He was now looking at Trudi Langmeijer, adding, 'And, yes, we were all aware of her family living close by.'

Trudi nodded her head, agreeing. 'She was on compassionate leave.'

'What's that?'

'Compassionate leave.'

'Evi was suffering fatigue,' interjected De Vos. 'She was in the fourth stage of lung cancer.'

Felly's eyes widened. She looked at her department colleagues, none of whom seemed to be surprised by such news.

The male policeman put away the small flipbook he was carrying. 'If any of you had been here earlier, we do have ways of checking, you know. Web cams, hotel guest lists, for example.'

'And why would we be lying?' Pascal huffed indignantly. 'Just exactly what do you suspect occurred?'

'We're still waiting on the medical examiner to release his report. Then again, this is only released to the family.'

He looked down, red-faced.

'I'd suggest you take it up with them.'

'Got it,' said Pascal, angrily.

'So, to be clear, everyone arrived yesterday and no one saw Evi Anneveldt beforehand, meaning Thursday...or Wednesday even, the day leading up to her death.'

All eyes were on the policewoman, shaking their heads, no.

'I was hoping to speak to her on Thursday,' said De Vos. 'I wanted to convince her to ride back with us after the seminar was over. She'd been gone all week and wasn't returning any calls.'

'And was there a reason for this?' asked the policewoman. 'Something that couldn't wait before seeing her at the conference?'

Felly caught his grey eyes darting again to Trudi before shaking his head, no. As she had nothing to hide, she thought to take the heat off her colleagues, adding, 'I went by Evi's house in Leiden before coming here yesterday. And, yes, there were no signs of life when I peered in the windows.'

'Why did you go by her house, madam?'

She shrugged. 'It's on my way to work. I just wanted to check and see for myself. But I hadn't known she was on compassionate leave. No one told me that. I knocked, even. Since there was no response, I got back on my bike and continued on to school.'

'I see, and would you and she have been getting in touch about anything in particular?'

De Vos shifted from one foot to the other. 'I'm the one who asked Professor van Vliet to check in on her. A favour is all.'

'Then let me rephrase my question, why would YOU be wanting to check in on her there, especially if you knew she was with family here?'

He shrugged. 'A personal matter, nothing more.'

The police officer handed her card to Baas. 'If you, or anyone in your team,' she said, looking to Felly, remembers anything more to help us further with our investigation please contact us immediately. We have little to go on for now and nothing to offer to satisfy the van de Meervenne family.'

Felly's eyes grew even wider now. 'Van de Meervenne? Any relation to Alety Goyaerts van de Meervenne?'

Most every local knew about the wife of the 16th century Dutch surrealist, Jheronimus Bosch. And Felly's thoughts leaped to the brochure she had picked up at the front desk of the Jheronimus Bosch Art Centre. The brochure had advertised Bosch's artistic notoriety in the following statement: 'Monsters, saints, magical beasts and fantasy creatures. You won't know where to look first.' She surveyed the room full of her colleagues, but it was the officer who interrupted her thoughts.

With a half-smile, he said, 'I don't know how directly they are related...if at all.'

5

One lone silver Peugeot SUV occupied the parking space above the grassy slope now outlined with police tape left fluttering against a willow tree that was rooted along the embankment of the Wilhelmina bridge, a bridge with its own interesting past. It is the third along the line of historical foot bridges that were built to cross the River Dommel and in walking distance to the city centre from the train station. The first was built in the late 19th century and named the Station Bridge because of its close proximity to the Den Bosch rail line. This was replaced after the First World War, which was a time when the Netherlands remained neutral, but the bridge needed serious renovation. The second replacement was blown up during the Second World War when heavy fighting between the allies and German occupiers broke out. This was temporarily replaced by a service bridge, which was also demolished while enemy troops attempted to cross it. The current Wilhelminabrug got its name from the Dutch queen, who became one of the richest European monarchs of her time through her own business savvy and industrial investments. When the Germans invaded Holland, Queen Wilhelmina fled to

England and ruled her government in exile. Though suffering from ill-health, she returned when the Netherlands was liberated and then abdicated the throne to her daughter, Juliana. Naming the bridge after Queen Wilhelmina was in honour of her involvement in the WWII Dutch Resistance.

Felly stopped and scanned the knoll on her way to the train station, stepping cautiously toward the area where the restaurant concierge had reported hearing a splash. She walked across the green embankment, eyeing the bridge while thinking that the police must have surely combed through the area already. What could they have found, if anything? She hadn't known the disorganised professor as well as some of her students, the eccentric woman's classes were always well-attended. Charisma was the charm played out everywhere in education. Personality could easily trump the pursuit of knowledge, especially at university level where students had more freedom to pick and choose their own course curriculum. Felly was well aware of the defects in her own nature, and her bias about Evi Anneveldt had been based on brief encounters where she had sized up the other who had barely given her the time of day, as if her whole life had depended on waiting for the next smoke. There was a difference, a fine line between analysing and evaluating, judging and finding fault.

The ride to Leiden took a little over an hour with a brief stopover in Amsterdam South before Felly could exit the train and cycle the rest of her way home. The smell of cooking was in the air when she entered the houseboat and threw off her pack. Kieran was in the middle of flapping jacks, as he called it, and pancakes he could cook edibly well.

'Home again, home again, jiggety jig!' she said, announcing her arrival. 'Do I smell pancakes?' A Ragdoll approached then flopped down and rolled around the floor, almost tripping her. The overgrown kittens were forever underfoot, and those who cared for them needed to be mindful. 'Kijk uit, Puk!' she scolded with a smile.

Kieran was in his cook's apron as he poked his head from the kitchen. "Hey you! Hungry?"

'Mama, mama!' said Femke. She rushed up, embracing skirt and leggings. 'Look what Papa bought me.' Felly caught sight of the tortoise shell and was relieved to see it was just a toy. 'Wonderful,' she said, hugging her daughter.

'I've got a stack of jacks with your name on it.'

Felly saw that a porcelain plate had been set on the table alongside an open box of powdered sugar. 'I am hungry, but I need to wash my hands first. What a bizarre weekend this has been, and I'm glad to be home.'

'Femke and I watched yesterday's broadcast together.' Kieran looked down at his smiling daughter as he slid three golden brown pancakes onto the plate. 'Our only thoughts were to have our Mams home.'

She smiled as she bit into the crispy cakes. 'Aw, thanks, you two. I never felt in any danger, considering that the crime rate in Den Bosch is almost nil. But I did find out some disturbing stuff.'

Kieran took a bite of one of her cakes, washing it down with the mug of coffee in hand, listening.

'It turns out that Evi Anneveldt had been visiting family on compassionate leave. She had stage four lung cancer.'

'Oh, that's just sad.'

61

'My best friends are Sander and Emma,' piped in Femke. 'Sander is always late for school. Emma gave me her red marker. See?'

Felly smiled at her daughter. 'I see. How nice of Emma.'

'Now let Mama eat her breakfast, poppie.'

'I'm gonna colour some more, Mama. Okay?'

'Okay.' Felly watched their little girl in pink sweats and mismatched top skip down the hall. Both cats followed, playfully nipping her heels. She turned back to Kieran. 'I'm still trying to wrap my brain around all this. Like, was there someone with Evi when she slipped and fell? And could she have been pushed off the embankment where she supposedly hit her head? But, if so, why? What could have possibly been a motive. And how could someone just let her drown like that?' She chewed the bite she had taken and took a sip of coffee, pondering.

'The Dommel runs into the Maas, doesn't it?'

'Yes, eventually.'

Kieran shook his head, his brows creasing. 'I've heard that the Dommel is four metres deep in that part of the canal, which is pretty deep, not to mention cold this time of year. So's, anything could have happened. An accidental drowning is quite possible, yes. Well, there's been nothing more on the news that ye haven't told me already. It'll be interesting yer hearing from the dean the medical examiner's report, which the family hopefully decides to release. I'm curious to find out what exactly happened, myself.'

She nodded her head. 'And what the police might know that they're not telling us.'

He sat down with her, taking another bite and drinking from his cup. 'What a thing, eh?'

62

'Yes, indeed.' She looked at her half-finished plate and suddenly lost her appetite, letting Kieran finish off the rest. 'What a thing, yes,' she repeated.

Felly was back in school the next morning, her students absorbed in table flip charts coloured in with circular pie graphs and plastered on sticky notes. They had divided themselves into teams; and, in the midst of the slight chaos of raised voices, they explained to her how their member lists and objectives were panning out.

'First, a wow, a big wow. But slow down,' she said, laughing. 'Team leaders? Let me chat with you first.'

Annemiek was wearing another white sweater, this one with a slight tinge of pink and pulled over a lacey purple dress. 'Shall I start?' she said.

'Please do.'

'So, we've decided how we want our set-up to be, which includes what we're calling 'sleuthhounds'.

'Sleuthhounds?'

'Yes, these are avatars that will enable us to log-in individually, though we're still using our names and student IDs to allow you to track us more easily.'

Felly grinned sheepishly, knowing how technically unsavvy she really was. 'Much appreciated.'

'Secondly,' interrupted Minke, still wearing her pinstriped jacket. 'We're designing our game to include a choice of skill level, but everybody begins at ground level and advances upward.'

Reinier piped in at this point. 'And these skill levels we're developing on a point system. Everyone begins with

20 skill points. These points can then be used to purchase the skills they want to learn.'

Felly's interest perked. 'Like what kind of skills?'

'We're in the process of designing an order form for that,' he said with a grin.

Annemiek picked up where he left off. 'A skill could be, for example, being good at some kind of prop.'

'Hmm.... Prop, meaning like a superpower?'

Reinier laughed. 'Sort of, yes. A prop could aid you in your understanding of certain things, like what they could mean in helping you decipher a clue.'

'And this is where we come in again,' said Annemiek. 'Lotte? Tell the professor about the handprint and writing analysis props. Oh, and, of course, the liar detector,' she said with a laugh.

Felly laughed with her. 'Lie detector, you mean?'

'No, liar detector. It'll help you with deciphering cons, character judging...things like that.'

'I'm still in the developing stage, though,' said a beaming Lotte.

Felly noted how the young woman's confidence had raised exponentially since they had last spoke.

'We're also working on developing cases where everyone is drafting what they think would be good start-ups before we try coming up with harder cases to solve.'

'Could you include some of the cold cases we've been working on then?'

'Sure, why not?'

'Oh, and Professor van Houten wants you to know that he'll be meeting with team two this afternoon,' said Reiner. 'He wants to discuss design and development with us.'

'That's super. What a relief he got involved in this project,' she replied. 'This is exactly what I had in mind. What this information sharing of ideas and knowledge exchange programme is all about.'

Annemiek was listening while twisting one of her hair extensions. 'You mean like it takes a village?'

Felly said, 'Exactly that, yes. We're social animals who work better in groups. Not with everything, of course. But our sharing with one another our perspectives and talents often helps more than hinders. There are just so many ways of looking at a puzzle.'

Reinier was rubbing his chin, a mannerism not unlike Pascal's, but his was clean shaven, not stubbled. 'Not all pieces fit, of course.'

'Of course. Which is why no man – or woman – is an island, if you'll excuse the old and rather trite expression.'

Reinier began humming the song as others joined in, snickering.

'All right, all right. I guess I deserve that. So, guys, I'm thrilled with all your progress. I can't wait to see how everything develops. You've simply bedazzled me. I'm not kidding when I say that you're awesome.'

They all beamed back at her, Reinier Nolten giving her the three-fingered salute. She saluted back, laughing.

6

The following day Felly met with Pascal to hear how the discussion with team two had gone. 'I think we've created a monster with this one,' he confided.

They were sitting outside on a café terrace sipping coffee, the turquoise in Felly's eyes catching fire in the sun. 'Whatever do you mean?'

'Take Reinier, for example. He wants to turn everything into some kind of dark matter super skills programme.'

She burst out laughing. 'Have you seen that 'John Wick' neo-noir action thriller?'

'The one with Keanu Reeves? Oh yeah. Who hasn't?'

'Well, I wouldn't have, not if my husband hadn't talked me into it. But I could just picture our grunge looking student as an extra.'

He laughed, nodding his head. 'Then there's Minke, his sidekick. She's keen on implementing what I'd call 'everyman's detective skills.''

Felly was laughing harder now. 'Everyman's?'

'You know? Like the man on the street who can pick a lock with a clothes pin and sliding credit card?'

'I wonder where they all get these ideas?'

'Watching too much Netflix is my guess.'

She snorted, shaking her head. 'It's actually Lotte and Annemiek you have to thank for what you're calling 'everyman's skills'.... Which should be 'every woman's', in their case. Did they explain to you their liar detector props?'

'No, I missed out on that.'

'And I'll leave it to them to explain it to you better. So, do you think they're actually going to make this happen? Are they anywhere near turning this *Whodunit!* into any semblance of a serious online game?'

'Time will tell, time and the space we need to give them to work it all out with a minimum of interference on our part.'

'They'll have no problem here with all their AI stuff. I just want to make sure they develop a healthy set of storylines. Most important for me, though, is that they're able to incorporate the analytic skills they've been learning all term.'

'Patience, grasshopper,' he said, grinning. 'After the first team solidifies the narrative and set-up, we'll have a clearer idea of how things are coming together...or apart.'

She sipped her latte, deep in thought. 'They specifically expressed how they want to make their narratives open-ended.'

'Why is that?' he said with interest.

'This way they're assuring me that not only individuals, but also pairs, and even groups, can participate in the interviews and questioning roleplay of the suspects that they're creating.'

He yawned, apologising immediately. 'Sorry, fresh air always has this effect on me.'

'You look tired, Pascal. Perhaps you should take in more sun. Vitamin D is good for you.'

'I know, I know.' He closed his eyes, soaking in the warm rays. 'I dread the oncoming winter. It's nice meeting like this, outdoors and away from all the bullshit of office politics and half-baked agendas of other well-meaning academics.'

'You mean like our new trends in education conference in Den Bosch?'

He laughed sardonically. 'Wasn't that so helpful?' And what about that blowhard of a guest speaker? Come on. Such a waste of department funding.'

'I can't say I don't agree with you, but talk like this could get us in trouble.'

'Nah, we're tenured. We don't go gently.'

'Not without a legal battle, at least.'

'Here's to teachers' unions.' He raised his cup to hers and finished his drink.

'I have a confession to make.'

'Which is?'

'When Reinier first proposed this idea of his, I was both intrigued and worried sick.'

'Like the feeling you get when sensing a headache coming on?'

She nodded her head, yes.

'I've had those, myself. It comes with the territory, don't you think? Of letting students take more risks?'

'Don't get me wrong. I do like the hands-on approach. They're so into it too, which is nice to see.'

'And what teaching's all about, the 'ah-hah' experience.'

'Whether it's going to be a success or a total disaster.'

'And you're quite the adventurous prof to allow them to do it.'

'I was more so when younger. I think having children tones down your risk-taking somewhat.'

'I can imagine. You now have someone other than just yourself to think about. How's that working for you, anyway?'

'What, the limited risk-taking?'

'No, the happy family thing.'

She sipped from her cup, absently checking the time. 'I've no regrets. Speaking of which...school's out, and I've got to cycle over and pick up my little monster.'

Pascal rose with her. 'I've always admired your lifestyle, Felly.'

'And you? Is there no one in your life, Pascal?'

He shook his head, no, eyeing her sheepishly. 'All the good ones are presently taken.'

She returned the sheepish grin, undaunted. 'You could get yourself into trouble with that look, especially from a jealous husband.'

'Like I said, presently taken.'

'On that note, let's meet again after both teams are further down the road with merging all their abstract ideas.'

'Okie doke.'

Both phones pinged just then, a general message from the department secretary. 'Hmm, I guess we'll be seeing each other sooner than later. I wonder what tomorrow morning's staff meeting is all about?'

Pascal frowned, shrugging his shoulders.

'Now I've really got to go. Femke gets upset when I'm late.'

'Till tomorrow then.' He watched her cycle off then straddled his own bike, heading in the other direction.

Femke was still too young to venture out on her own and still relied on both parents to take turns accompanying her with their own bikes on her way to school. She was in what the Dutch call the first class of her international school, which could be comparable to an English nursery school, or kindergarten. And, on this particular day, all the pre-schoolers and primary classes were abuzz with festivities to celebrate the Germanic region of Europe's Saint Nicholas Day. The mysterious 'Sinterklaas' didn't appear through chimney tops mostly because typical Dutch rowhouses didn't include hearths in their architecture. Also known as 'Santa Claus' to the English and Americans, this patron saint banged at children's front doors after riding through the evening dusk upon his horse, Amerigo. Alongside him were the 'black-face' helper-Piets, who were causing recent controversy because of their symbolic history that was rooted in the slave-trade, a darkly lucrative endeavour of Holland's sea merchant past with the Dutch East India Company. These days the Piets in costume were mostly ashen-faced, as if dusted by soot though, again, Dutch chimneys were few and far between.

Family celebrations of Saint Nicholas Day included open invitations to relatives who didn't mind waiting out the anticipated event with offered drinks and snacks, such as beer, wine, gin and 'bitterballen', a spicy meatball eaten as an hors d'oeuvre. Felly and her twin, Filip, had fond memories awaiting the arrival of Saint Nicholas and his bag full of toys. When in their teens, they still played along, but mostly with comical gags that the helper-Piets were known to play. And, as adults, it was especially nice to have all the gift giving done by the Fifth of December which allowed for the rest of the holiday to be enjoyed with festive gatherings of wining and dining one another to lessen the sting of the approaching dreariness of winter.

Felly cycled right up to the schoolyard and stopped when she caught sight of her daughter racing across the asphalt with a large, bulging sock decorated with stitched bows and stencilled snowflakes.

'Look Mama!' cried Femke excitedly. 'Teacher made us hang these silly socks at school and Sinterklaas put candy in them, not in my shoes.'

'Maybe because you're wearing them, yes?'

She looked down at her black laced ankle boots. 'Yes.'

'Does this mean that we won't see the Saint tonight then?'

Lips forming into a pout, Femke suddenly eyed her drooping sock with disdain.

'Oh, poppie. Such a face. Mama's just teasing you. I'm sorry.'

She brightened immediately. 'I made a riddle, too! Zwarte Piet says: 'What's black and white and red all over?'

Felly wrinkled up her nose. 'Hm, that's a hard one. A zebra sticking out its tongue?'

Giggling, 'Pip and Puk eating strawberries!'

'Oh, that's funny! Now hop on your bicycle and we'll go do some shopping before Papa gets home. What would you like for dinner? Something simple, please. Oma and Opa are coming over later to celebrate with us.'

'Pannenkoeken!'

'Of course,' she said, grinning. 'Why even ask?'

72

And what child didn't like them? Kieran could fry them up too while she prepared for their evening guests. After dinner, Femke would get what every Dutch child traditionally got on this eve, a bar of chocolate formed into the first letter of her name. Adult drinks would include 'advocaat', which consisted of brandy liqueur blended with egg yolk, sugar, and a touch of vanilla. Bitterballen, nuts, cheese and crackers were also laid out on hors d'oeuvre platters.

Not wanting the Ragdolls to be left out of the festivities, Femke insisted that feline treats be included in the grocery items. With shopping done and tucked away in saddle bags, they pedalled off in the form of transportation used in Holland the way people in other countries would use their cars. Cycling was second nature to the Dutch from the moment one could reach the pedals. Even age-old seniors were seen everywhere on their bikes, as were Felly's parents who were now in their late 60s.

'Home again, home again, jiggety jig,' they sang in top volume, feeling the breeze in their hair and holiday spirit while cycling home. This was followed by, in Dutch, 'We zijn er bijna, we zijn er bijna, maar nog niet helemaal.'

When arriving, Femke opened the houseboat's sliding door for her mother, who had bags in her arms. Then she rushed in and scolded the little cats, who had knocked down some Christmas balls and were rolling them across the parquet floor. Puk was even carrying a wooden star in his mouth. 'Stoute poezen! Naughty cats!' she cried.

Felly set the bags on the counter and picked up the ornaments. 'They're just cats being cats, poppie.'

'But, Mama, they're ruining the decorations.'

'Which is also why we now have LED lights instead of plug-ins. We don't want to shock the little devils.'

Femke eyed the cats suspiciously. 'No treats for bad cats.'

'Now go put on your play clothes. I need to do some things in the kitchen to get ready for Oma and Opa coming over.

'Are Tante and Oom coming too?'

'I hope so, but it'll all be after dinner, liefje. So, go get changed.'

Femke skipped off to her room with the Ragdolls trailing behind. Kieran entered the houseboat just then and placed an almond-filled pastry log atop the kitchen counter then plopped a kiss on Felly's cheek. 'Happy Sinterklaas! A gift from HR. I stopped by the liquor store too. You wouldn't believe how hard it is to find this bloody stuff. So, I bought two pints. Thank you very much, Gall and Gall.'

Felly picked up one of the bottles he was referring to. 'Mm, chocolate Baileys. Shall I pour us a taste?'

'It's bloody Christmas, yes. Sinterklaas Day, I mean. Everything goes while waitin' for them Dutch leprechauns.'

'Zwarte Pieten?' She leaned across the counter and kissed his frozen nose, smiling. It was then she noticed the somewhat squashed looking Poinsettia plant next to his battered leather briefcase.

'Oh, yeah.' He shot her a boyish grin. 'And a Christmas rose for me rose...a little worse for wear after the bike ride. But it'll perk up again.'

'Why, how lovely. I'll get the glasses if you set it on the table.' She took out two crystal flutes from a small kitchen cupboard and poured in the dark milky liqueur. 'Proost.'

Femke burst out from her room just then, cats still on her heels. 'Papa, papa!' Kieran set down his glass to hug his daughter. 'You smell like chocolate,' she said, smelling his breath.

'Guilty as charged. And how 'bout me flappin' some jacks for my little girl?'

'Mm, lekker.'

'Hagelslag on yers too?'

She nodded her head up and down. 'Joey doesn't even know what hagelslag means. Can you believe it?'

'No!' said Kieran, feigning shock. 'So's who's this Joey? Someone I need to worry about?'

She giggled. 'No, papa.'

'And what did ye tell this illiterate young'un?'

'I told him that they're chocolate sprinkles, of course.'

'And who doesn't know that?'

'Joey says he only knows about putting syrup on pancakes, like his Nan gives him. She's from London. Is that where Pip and Puk come from?'

'Our cats come from Leeuwarden, due north of us. London is in England. Bring the iPad over after dinner and we'll look it up together.'

'He doesn't even know what hagelslag tastes like.'

'Imagine that.'

'And, and Joey doesn't speak Dutch.'

'Oh?' Felly frowned, interjecting. 'I thought everyone in your class spoke Dutch.'

'And I said he should learn 'cause he lives here now.'

'It's nice of ye to speak English to him.'

She looked up at her father, shrugging her shoulders.

'And is this Joey lad from London too?'

'He says he's from Barking.'

Kieran grinned at her. 'Barking mad, is he?'

She giggled and plucked a few sprinkles from the pancake he just made her, placing them on her tongue.

'We can look up Barking too, but only after dinner.' Kieran turned back to his wife, saying, 'A detective stopped by the office today.'

'Oh? And?'

'He spoke to my colleague about the woman in yer department who drowned. It's possible she wasn't alone when she fell and hit her head. They think the head injury is how she ended up drowning in the canal.'

Her interest perked. 'Why do they suspect someone else might have been with her?'

He shrugged. 'I was only eavesdroppin' and couldn't ask. I also overheard there were excessive amounts of alcohol and drugs in her system. It was in her toxicology report.'

'Hm, maybe suicide? I don't know about the drink, though the drugs could be explained by her cancer. I'm sure stage four lung cancer is quite painful.'

Kieran nodded his head. 'I wouldn't wish it on anyone, that's for sure.'

'But if someone were with her, they could've saved her from drowning. My God, Kieran, how cruel would that be? Standing there watching her drown.'

'Mind yerself around that lot, darlin'.'

'Technically they're another department, though we're all under the shared umbrella of humanities these days in this cross-curriculum trend of shared learning. One of their professors, in fact, is currently co-managing a capstone project with me.'

'Oh?' He raised a brow.

'Yes, our serious gaming project.' She eyed him sidewise. 'Why? Are you jealous, Kier?'

'Not a'tal, but ye can't blame me for being a little uncomfortable after hearing about this woman's death.'

'I'm careful, believe me.'

'I know, I know. But I never trust the other guy. So, shall I flap ye a jack?'

'I'm good. Thanks.'

'Seriously, yer all gathered under one roof, but ye still don't know those people, nor what they're capable of.'

'I'm working with professors, not criminals.'

'Even professors have their quirks. I should know, I married one.'

She laughed. 'What's that supposed to mean?'

'That curiosity killed the cat, and ye are a very curious woman. Oh, and, please, don't share this information I told you with anyone.'

'You know what I don't get, Kier? What Evi was doing there so late in the first place? That's what I'd like to know. Oh, to be a fly on the wall, eh?'

'Or, in her case, an airborne drone.'

'And today I got a message that Dr Ernie wants to meet up with everyone tomorrow. I wonder what that's all about?'

'Maybe he's got the medical report and can shed some light on all this.'

You'll be home in the morning, yes? I'm sure it won't take long.'

He nodded his head. 'No problem, and I think that yer dean is smart to include you all.'

'To minimise the gossip?'

He raised his glass. 'Curiosity killed the cat, as I said. So, kill the curiosity in the first place and mind the cat. Sláinte.'

She downed the rest of her glass, saying, 'I'd best get those bitterballen made before the parents come round with Filip and Moira.'

'Need any help, mo stór?' He rose, resting his cheek on hers.

She stood momentarily still, enjoying the feel of skin made smooth from a morning shave. 'No, liefje' she purred. 'How about later, when all is done and the guests are gone?'

'That's a date.' Then he turned to his daughter, her face now smeared in chocolate. 'Enjoying yourself, poppie?'

The little girl smiled, chocolate between her teeth.

'So, tell me more about this wayward classmate.'

'What's a 'way wart', papa?'

'That's a warthog losing his way home. When I was just yer age, we saw them scampering all over the village. Once after a big pouring rain I found one playing with a leprechaun at the end of a rainbow.'

Femke's mouth dropped, her eyes widening.

'Stop it, Kieran,' chided Felly. 'You know she hangs on your ever word.'

'Aw, what's the fun of childhood then?'

'Lots, but not filling your own with stuff and nonsense.'

'Now, look, poppie. Mama has spoken. I promise not to speak anymore about silly Irish leprechauns this evening. Instead, we'll concentrate on Sinterklaas and Zwarte Piet.'

Felly shot him a sidewise grin. 'Point taken.'

He winked at Femke, brushing off imaginary dust. 'So's...what's the old Saint bringing in that sack of his tonight?'

'Dream Spirit ponies!' she squealed out.

'Phew,' muttered Felly, thinking how glad she was

to have included that on the list of toys she'd bought. Then she turned back to the spicing up of the Dutch meatballs.

When the family arrived, Femke had her teeth brushed and was already in pyjamas and running around the room on a sugar high.

'And how's our little darlin' this evenin', said Moira, seeing Kieran and Felly resting on the couch, drinks in hand. She went into the kitchen with her oliebollen, which was a type of powdered donut ball she'd learnt to make while living in the Netherlands. 'Well, look at ye, ye muppet. Waiting for the old saint?'

Femke nodded her head. 'Any minute now, I feel my bones.'

'Ye feel yer bones?'

'Yes,' she said, skipping around the room. 'My bones.'

Felly rolled her eyes, saying, 'She ate her whole chocolate letter.'

'Ah, but doesn't everything smell delightful. And I just brought a wee bit of something extra.'

'You shouldn't have, Moira. There's so much here already.'

The other woman glimpsed the small living room table that was festively arranged with seasonal hors d'oeuvres. 'Just a wee bit of nothin', she said. 'Filip tells me ye can't celebrate the holidays without includin' them oily balls, am I right?'

Felly laughed aloud as her twin walked in and gave her the traditional three kisses, one on each cheek and an extra for good measure. 'What's so funny?'

'Oh, just oily balls.' Felly laughed harder.

He grinned, raising a hand. 'Not going there. So, how's life in the down under, Sis?' A private joke beginning when he and Moira moved to a rowhouse closer to their parents in Leiden's older residential section north of the university.

'Can't complain, Bro. Life is chill here in the canals.'

'And will Sinterklaas be riding this evening, or is it just Zwarte Piet with his switch? I hear the cats have been especially naughty this year.'

Femke pointed to the kittens now batting around another fallen Christmas star. 'He's coming for me, not them.'

Filip snorted, grinning widely.

'Hey brother,' greeted Kieran. 'What'll ye have? Pick yer poison.'

'A full shot of something strong and hard.'

'Whiskey it is then. And, Moira?'

She eyed the bottle of Bushmills Black Label he was pouring in a glass for Filip. 'So, where's yer Paddy's, Cork man?'

'Is it Paddy's for ye then?'

She took a sip of her husband's drink, nodding her approval. 'Yer grand. This'll do nicely.'

'Good, 'cause the Paddy's is tucked safely under the toilet lid.'

She clinked his glass. 'And I'll be sure and remember that the next time I'm asked to babysit.'

Felly's parents entered just then through the sliding glass door, her father holding bottles of wine and Jenever. 'We hear a party going on. Are we invited?'

'Yers is always an open invitation,' said Kieran. 'But, here, let me help you.'

'Always come prepared,' said Martinus. 'I forgot the tonic, though. Do you have any?'

'We do, I'll just get that for ye. And some Pinot Noir, Ankie?'

'Please,' said Felly's mother, smiling. 'Felly, schat, these bitterballen are delicious. I taste red pepper.'

'Yes, I wanted to make the recipe spicier this time.'

A sudden pounding at the rarely used front door, caused a momentary silence from deck to kitchen. Then a five-year-old's gasping was heard.

'He's here,' whispered Femke. She clung to the leggings of her mother's leisurewear as her father opened the door and peered out.

'Are ye there, Saint Nick?' Kieran waved to the neighbours; the couple he'd arranged to leave a sack full of toys by the door. They returned the wave and whisked up the landing to their own houseboat that was moored close by. 'Jayz,' he said, 'that ol' Nick is quick, quick as a wink.'

'Did he leave anything for me?' squealed the excited child.

'Let's have a look.' He peered further. 'What's this?' He lugged in a canvas sack as everyone gathered round and expressed feigned astonishment. Inside were ribbon-tied packages of items collected throughout the year. Gift wrapped socks and leggings with matching sweaters mixed in with wish-list items, such as the Spirit Riding Free barn and horse set that Femke wanted. A 'Bake with Me' oven set came from her aunt and uncle. And a warm and snug winter coat in pretty pink had been purchased by her grandparents.

'What do you say?' said Felly to her delighted daughter.

'Dank je wel, Sinterklaas...thank you, thank you. Can I play with everything now?'

'Pick one thing out of the pile, then off to bed.'

'Hmm, I pick Abigail and her horse, Boomerang.'

'The rest you can play with in the morning.'

She grabbed the horse and doll, holding them tightly to her chest as everyone kissed her goodnight. 'Oh,' she said suddenly. 'I forgot to give Pip and Puk their treats.'

Felly looked around but only heard sounds of rattling Christmas decor. 'You can give the treats to them tomorrow. Right now, I want you to brush your teeth. Then you can read to me your book about the cow who fell into the canal.'

'Okay, Mama.'

'I'll be in in a minute. So, get ready now.'

Felly soon entered her child's room and slid in-between the crisp white sheets and duvet covered in floral designs. She snuggled up close as Femke opened a book and began reading one of her favourite stories. 'While visiting a large city, Hendrika, the Dutch cow,' pausing. 'What's this word, Mama?'

'Ac-ci-den-tal-ly. Hendrika didn't mean to fall in. It was by accident.'

'Askuhdentluhy...Hendrika didn't mean to fall in a canal and floated gently down the stream.' Femke's eyelids drooped, and the book slid from the grasp of little fingers.

Her mother took over as the child listened to the more mature but soft, singsong voice. Felly turned the page and read on. 'Hendrika's adventures began,' she read, 'with a raft that just happened to be floating by.' And, as she read, Felly thought of another who'd fallen into a canal. But there was no magical raft. Perhaps only someone who may have callously watched her drown.

82

7

Saturday's meeting with Dean Huijsman was an informal weekend gathering, everyone showing up in their street clothes. Winter coats, scarves and hats were left hanging on an overburdened coat rack by the department entrance, early December weather turning suddenly cold and nasty with grey skies and a chilling wind that bit you to the bone.

Felly was wearing blue jeans and a long, heavy green sweater. Her knitted scarf she simply untied and left fashionably draped around her as she waited with the others. She took a sip of the coffee she had poured and let its steam rise to tickle her frost-bitten nose as she watched with everyone else as Dr Ernie read excerpts of the copy of the medical examiner's statement that Evi's family, the van de Meervennes, had sent him. Regardless of rumours, hers had been determined a non-suspicious death, a death by drowning occurring in a natural manner.

'But what about the suspected...?' Felly blurted out before swallowing the tail-end of her sentence. Kieran had told her not to mention his insider information.

'What was that, Felly?' said the dean.

She breathed out. 'What I meant to say is that this can't be all there is to it. The splash was heard well after midnight. This was no casual stroll.'

'Be that as it may,' Ernie said, 'this is the official conclusion.'

'And an easy one for the authorities,' interjected Pascal, rolling his eyes. 'I for one have heard nothing about the supposed investigation other than a lack of transparency from the police.'

The dean shook his head and shrugged. 'This is all I know, Pascal. I'm sorry. Evi's loss will be deeply felt. It's been a sad time for all of us, and the family tells me they have no objection to anyone wanting to attend the memorial service. Details will follow in an email sent by our staff secretary.'

Felly shot a sidewise glance at the uncomfortably smiling Trudi. The others in the room looked chagrined, except for Pascal, who turned from everyone, jaw tightening, squeezing and blinking his eyes.

'I'm sad for your department's loss, Pascal. Were you and Dr Anneveldt close?'

'Want to get out of here and get a real coffee?' he asked her.

She set down her half full cup. 'Sure, where to?'

'Cafeteria's fine with me.'

She gave him a brief nod and followed out the door.

'Cappuccino?' he said at the order counter.

'Uh, latte for me, please. So, what do I think you're not telling me?'

He paid then motioned to an empty couch. There he sat, taking a breath before choking out, 'Evi Anneveldt was my birthmother.'

'What?' She caught her drink she was about to spill.

'You know I was adopted, right?'

'No, I didn't know that. But go on.'

'My parents adopted me at birth.' He took a sip of his cappuccino. 'Nothing unusual there. I had a normal childhood growing up with a keen interest in history and science. Only later did I become curious about anthropology, its cultural aspects more than the digs. And the clinical part of my graduate studies continued here, interning in our very department. I stayed on and on. The path laid out for me seeming so easy to follow. Now I'm wondering if luck had anything to do with it.'

'Meaning that Evi could have pulled some strings? She being.... How could she be your mother?'

He set down his cup and rested his head in his hands. 'I never knew she was. Not until yesterday when I received a letter from the van de Meervennes. Her family had decided to contact me.'

'Jesus, Pacal. Seriously? How big of them. What a thing to find out... And incredibly horrible timing on their part.'

'I know, I know. Believe me when I say that my mind is completely blown too.'

'And what about your adopted parents? Why hadn't they told you all this beforehand?'

'They told me all right, when I was old enough to understand...about eleven, I think.'

'I thought you said you just found out.'

'My parents didn't know who my birthmother was. It wasn't disclosed at the adoption. And, yes, they were as dismayed as I was when I showed them the letter.'

'You live at home?'

85

He fidgeted with his drink. 'I had a partner for several years and only last summer decided to call it quits. It was a congenial split, but I was admittedly the one packing my bags. I really should get my own place, yes. Just not today. Maybe in a few tomorrows. Yeah, tomorrow sounds good to start looking around again.'

'It does save a lot of money living at home. But I think my parents would drive me crazy after a week.'

'Mine aren't that bad, really. We get along fine.'

'Mine are wonderful too, but.... Anyway, I've got my own household now with husband and five-year-old daughter, not to mention our two obnoxious kittens.'

He smiled at her. 'Sounds idyllic.'

'And what's the rush? You're in your twenties. Students adore you.'

'No rush. And students don't think too badly of you either. I mean, this serious gaming project has been an ingenious course capstone.'

'It was Reiner Nolten's brain child. I just gave the go ahead, and they're all teaching me a lot about IT in the process. Yet, I don't think we could have launched this without some strong support on your part. Your input has been very helpful.'

'Yeah, it's been fun. Anyway, I thought I should explain this bizarre connection of mine with Evi Anneveldt.'

'Wow, just wow.' She eyed him curiously. 'And you had no inkling at all until this letter?'

'None whatsoever. What the fuhk, heh?'

'Yeah. Like, why did she give you up for adoption in the first place? And now that she's gone, she can never explain to you why she did what she did.'

Pascal drained his cup. 'Do you really think her drowning was just an accident, Felly?'

86

She rose from the couch and threw her empty cup in the bin. 'Now it doesn't matter what I think, not after the medical examiner's official report.'

She saw anger in his eyes when he looked at her. 'No,' he said. 'I guess it really doesn't.'

'So, I have an idea. How about following me home? That is, if you're free this afternoon. My husband's a defence attorney and maybe we could get him to shed some professional light on this, see what we're not seeing. Or, maybe not. I don't know. It's worth a try. Yes?'

'Obnoxious kittens, you say? What are they? Tabby?'

'They're Ragdolls.'

'Ragdolls? I'm not familiar with the breed. Are they like a Persian? My parents had one when I was growing up...along with a Chow. Lots of fur.'

'They're an official American breed, but I think they're a cross between Siamese and Persian. And the ragdoll name comes from their odd characteristic that, when you pick them up, they flop in your arms like a ragdoll.'

He laughed. 'Sounds interesting.'

'They're still kittens, so quite the handful. And along with a pre-schooler? Well, let me just confess to you beforehand that my current household situation is somewhat chaotic and not to everyone's taste.'

'Okay,' he said with a grin. 'I'm game. If anything, it sounds like a pleasant distraction.'

Pascal sized up the houseboat on the Rijnkade canal with admiration when they cycled up to the embankment. 'I had no idea you were one of these people.'

'And what type of people are you referring to? River rats?' she teased.

'Hardly. Yours is a beautiful structure. Does she have a name?'

'We call her 'de Zwaan'.'

'Well, she's nice and long like a longnecked swan, but the name is not too original.'

She grinned at his frankness. 'It was mostly my daughter's doing. She was a few years younger at the time we moved house. Which was an upgrade for us, believe me. And the first thing she noticed was the swans floating up river. She kept pointing at them and repeating the name. Thus, our christening her 'the Swan'...our boat, not our Femke,' she said with a chuckle.

He continued looking around as she instructed him to chain his bike to the pole alongside hers. 'I like the blue panelling,' he went on. 'The colour really offsets the white trim all around. I'm envious.'

She smiled and motioned to the deck. 'After you.' He climbed on and entered with her through the sliding glass door. Kieran was sitting at the front room table when they came in. His laptop open and papers strewn everywhere as he ticked on a handheld calculator, stopping and looking up only when he caught sight of them out of the corner of his eye.

Pascal went immediately over and extended a hand. 'Pascal,' he said. 'I hope I'm not interrupting anything.'

'Not a'tal. Paperwork's the one thing I don't like about the job, any job.'

'Hey, you're talking to teachers.'

This was Felly's cue to introduce them to each other. 'My husband, Kieran,' she said. 'And, Kier, Pascal is the one working with me on the serious gaming project.'

'So, how's that going for ye?'

'So far it's going good. Your accent, are you Irish?'

He broke into a grin. 'I hope that's not a crime.'

'Not in any of my circles. How long have you been living in the Netherlands?'

'Long enough to butcher yer language and not to repeat any of my shameful Dutch in mixed company if I can help it.'

'Our language is not so difficult. Right, Felly?'

'Well, it is our native tongue.'

'At least I find it easier than English with all those exceptions to the rules.'

'Try speaking Irish,' she said.

'Thank you, no. I like the sound of it, though. There's something old and ancient about Gaelic.'

Kieran smiled as Felly's eyes trailed down the hallway. 'Is Femke in her room? I think I hear sounds of her playing with Pip and Puk.'

'The obnoxious cats, I presume?'

'And one small fry of the human pod version.' Kieran rose and went into the small kitchen refrigerator. 'What's yer poison, Pascal?'

'What have you got? I like most anything as long as it's cold and fresh.'

'For me that'll be a Murphy's or a shot of whiskey. Felly prefers wine. We've got both, red and white.'

'I'll take that shot of whiskey, please.'

'Paddy's it is.' He came back with a dram glassful of straw-gold ale. He had opened a bottle of amber beer for himself and a flute of red wine for Felly. '

Pascal took the offered glass. 'Cheers, proost and sláinte. That's all I know.'

'Sláinte mhat,' said Kieran, drinking his ale.

Pascal's eyes scanned the ruffled living quarters, letting the mellow taste of fermented grain roll around his tongue just as a barefooted child with lipstick smears all over her face appeared out of one of the back rooms.

'Oh no, poppie, really?' said mother to daughter. 'Did you get into Mama's lipstick again?'

The little girl shook loose blonde curls highlighted red in the sun. Then she pointed to two of the prettiest white and blue-mittened cats that Pascal had ever seen. 'I only gotsta see what Pip was playing with.'

'I hope it's only on your face and not on the walls.'

'No way, that's baby stuff,' she said in a huff.

'Excuse me for a moment. I just need to go take a peek.' Felly took her glass as her daughter followed with her into the backroom.

'Have a seat,' said Kieran. He cleared off a stack of paper to make space for the guest. 'So, how'd the briefing go? What a thing to happen, eh?'

'No need to repaint any walls just yet,' said Felly returning with a look of relief.

Both men grinned up at her, Pascal saying, 'Kieran just asked how the briefing went. According to the coroner it's now an official accident.... I guess.'

'An official accident?'

Felly nodded her head. 'The family sent Dean Huijsman a copy of the medical examiner's statement.'

Pascal added, 'Which Dr Ernie summarised by saying it was death by accidental drowning.'

'Well, there you have it. Not pretty, but case closed.'

Felly's eyes locked on Kieran's. 'What about...? Well, other possible evidence?'

Kieran eyed her back, saying, 'A dreadful thing. But with no clear evidence of foul play...?' He shrugged his shoulders.

'Can I see you in the kitchen for a minute, Kier?'

'Excuse us, Pascal.' He rose from his chair and followed her in. 'I know what you're doing, darlin'. But what I told ye in confidence is only hearsay and not to be shared with yer man over there.'

'I haven't given away any secrets just yet. But I thought, well, he just found out that Evi was his mother.'

'Say that again?'

'His birthmother, yes. Poor man.'

He shot a glance into the next room, sizing the other man up, his eyes looking back at her sadly. 'I'm sorry, darlin'. If I had anything concrete to share I would. But I don't.'

'Can't you somehow look into this a bit more? Help me out, would you?'

'Oh, Felly,' he sighed. 'Didn't I warn ye not to get involved?'

'He's my colleague, Kieran. How could I not?' They re-entered the room, neither exactly happy with the other.

'Are ye thinking then that the death might not have been an accident?' Kieran said to Pascal.

'He's thinking,' said Felly, repeating what she'd said in the kitchen, 'that now he knows who Evi Anneveldt is, was, meaning his mother, and I'm thinking too.... Well, could someone else have wanted her to keep mum?'

'But who? Who else would care but me?' Pascal was exasperated. 'And I only just found out.'

Kieran eyed the other man with caution, letting him continue.

'We all knew about her cancer and request for compassionate leave. She even dropped by my office and asked if I'd cover some of her courses.'

'And why didn't she tell you then that she was your mother?' said Felly. 'Sorry, Pascal, but I think the woman was heartless.'

'Yes, she was. And we'd been working alongside each other all this time. You think she could at least have had the decency to tell me then.'

'At the very least, yes. It would have been the decent thing for her to do.'

'I can't explain it, Felly. Yet, in her defence, she did ask to meet up after the conference, saying she wanted to explain a few things. At the time, I just thought it was her illness and gratitude for my taking on some of her coursework, perhaps even later on a more permanent basis. But that was all. I had no idea she might have been wanting to discuss her being my....' He stopped, his voice cracking.

'Pascal?' she said suddenly. 'Who else was in the department at the time? Who else might have overheard you and her talking together?'

'There was no one within earshot. We were in my office and the door was closed...by her, I might add.'
'How about Baas? Could he have overheard you? Those office walls aren't so thick.'

'Who's Baas?' said Kieran.

'Sorry, Baas, his boss, Sebastian De Vos.'

Pascal said, 'The head of my division.'

'Oh, right. The one who wanted you to check on her house.'

'He did? I wonder why.'

'Me too, Pascal. Now more than ever.'

'Don't go jumping to any half-baked conclusions. They may only muddy the waters, darlin'.'

'I won't Kier. I'm only thinking out loud.' She reached over and ruffled his hair. 'But seriously, when I asked Pascal to follow me home, I was hoping you might offer some fresh insight.'

'Okay, then. Let's assume Evi wasn't alone when she died...and I'm stressin' 'assume'. There could have been visible footprints on the knoll, which is a public area. It would be difficult to single out a suspect even if footprints were in plain view. Also, since it was well into the wee hours when the splash was reported, the following morning's weather, meaning dew, might have just as easily erased them, that kind of thing. I know the police would've investigated any and all evidence they had found. Yet, you see the difficulty of finding plausible evidence.'

'I see,' said Pascal.

'But if there was something else....'

Felly leaned into him. 'Like a witness who might have heard voices?'

'Exactly. A witness, a piece of torn clothing. Was there anything else the police found? Do you know?'

Felly glanced at Pascal, who shrugged in response. 'Could you ask, Kier? You're over at the police station all the time.'

'At the main Leiden station, yes. But this would be a Den Bosch matter. Even so, how forthcoming do you think they'd be? I may be a lawyer, but I don't represent anyone, especially now that you say the case has been concluded.'

'Hmm, I wonder,' she said.

Kieran raised a brow. 'Wonder what?'

'If anything might have been found...or missed.'

'Personals collected on the scene would go back to the family. You say that you now have a connection to this family via their letter?'

'Yes, but I don't know them at all.'

'I see,' said Kieran. 'Well, that's unfortunate.'

'An accident is understandably possible,' Felly went on. 'Except that it was her head bump that allowed her to drown in those waters.'

He looked at his wife. 'Slipping, falling and hitting one's head. Sad, but these types of accidents happen all the time.'

'You're right, they do. Which brings us back to the initial question: What was Evi Anneveldt doing on that embankment in the middle of a chilly night?'

Pascal interjected. 'If only the dead could talk.'

'And we're back to square one,' said Kieran.

Pascal finished his whiskey and eyed his watch. 'It was nice meeting you, and...' He looked around. 'Seeing your lovely houseboat.' He shook the other man's hand again. 'I also appreciate you sparing the time to hear me out.'

'I'm sorry I couldn't be more of a help to you. I'm sure it's understandably frustratin'.'

'I'm honestly beginning to care less and less about the woman. As far as her being on that knoll in the middle of the night? Well, she did have stage four lung cancer, which alone would cause untold anxiety. Perhaps she was just out for some air. And with the heavy medications she was on, I could easily imagine her slipping and falling on her own account.'

Kieran agreed. 'That could explain the mishap.'

Pascal turned to his colleague. 'As for our project setup, I think that students will be ready on Monday for a mock trial. Shall we run it through with you then?'

'Yes, I can't wait. I'll walk you to the door, Pascal.'

When Felly returned, she said, 'He looked so downcast.'

Kieran shook his head. 'I couldn't even imagine hearing about your birthmother like that. What an itch.'

'An itch?'

'With a capital 'B'.

She smiled at that. 'And I don't for a minute believe that he doesn't care. I imagine he feels betrayed more than anything.'

'Can't say I blame him. So, mo chroí, what's for dinner? Are ye cooking this evening?'

'Oh, Kieran, really?'

'What? What'd I say?'

'Okay, how about fish sticks? They're easy to bake.'

'Sounds good to me.'

Femke came out just then. 'Is that man gone yet?'

'He is,' said Kieran. 'So, go wash up now.'

'Fish sticks, Mama? Are you making fish sticks?'

'I am, indeed.'

'Fish sticks, yummy!'

Felly watched her daughter skip into the washroom. 'You are two of a kind,' she said to Kieran. 'You and your mini-me...in female form.'

On Monday morning, students met with both Felly and Pascal where they performed a mock trial of the *Whodunit!* programme they had sublabelled the 'Hounds of

LU'. A small group of players was involved in the setup, their avatars appearing at the bottom of the screen with collected skill sets and tallies. The tallying of skills showed up on the left side of the gameboard. And, for this trial, the students had the game app playing out on an iPad. They were also quick to point out that the app could be loaded on a mobile as well.

It was Lotte who introduced the game. She blew a whisp of flaxen hair out of her eyes while beckoning to her classmate. 'As Minke will demonstrate,' she said, 'the goal is to show how easy it is to learn this game. Yet, it's still challenging because of the ability to pick and choose different crime-solving strategies.'

'Which,' interjected Annemiek, 'depends on the given narrative. Right, Lucas? He worked on these with me,' she told her professors.

Lucas bobbed his head, his side-parted pompadour nodding with him. And Reinier picked up the slack by pointing out a way to allow additional cases to be added as the game progressed.

'The players,' he said, 'compete with each other in teams who use the skill sets they've been collecting. These skills, if I can draw your attention to them, are shown on the left side. See here on this tally sheet?'

Minke continued on. 'Please note how the players can collect them, as they are point-based. And this begins with a base number of points to cash in to purchase an initial skill. That's just to motivate a person, to get them engaged. And, when a clue is used, if proven accurate, then more points are added to the team's avatars.

The final scores,' added Annemiek, 'are calculated when a mystery is solved. And the winners have a badge added to their avatar to show that they've solved a crime.

She tugged on her lacey sweater as she went on to say they had set up the game in this way so not just one player would win. 'It'll always be a team effort,' she said with a grin. 'Teams work on their cases interactively.'

Lotte piped in, concluding, 'The beauty of this is that you can add more and more cases to solve. They can be simple, or they can be complex, while using the critical thinking skills you've taught us.'

'Hurrah!' said Pascal, turning to Felly. 'So, now do you want to see, Professor?'

'Sure, Professor...and students. Shall we begin by saying the obvious?'

He laughed. 'You mean, the game's afoot?'

She smiled, stopping herself from replying, *No shit, Sherlock!*

Pascal went on to explain how teams consisted of four players per session, and each player would join in using their own devices. Felly watched with keen interest as her two more gregarious students, Reinier and Minke, began the mock trial. They chose the narrative: *Murder by Travel*, similar in thought to Agatha Christie's *Murder on the Orient Express*, where four individuals were being blackmailed by another who'd been murdered while all travelling together on a train, the Orient Express. Yet, it was Annemiek and Lotte's ghost team who demonstrated how a series of clues would result in the solving of the crime.

'Well done and well-played, everyone,' said Felly. 'So, besides completing your capstone project, what have you learnt here?'

Minke said, 'The importance of team work, most definitely.'

'And that everyone has a voice,' included Lucas.

Both Annemiek and Lotte were nodding their heads. 'I confess that I couldn't initially see how I'd be able to contribute to this,' Lotte added. 'Then I saw how other components, such as creating a storyboard of narratives, were also essential. And I didn't even need to be strong in IT skills.'

'Yes,' agreed Annemiek. 'We pretty much left that all up to Reinier and Minke.'

Reinier beamed. 'We also learnt that there's a market for this.'

Felly glimpsed Pascal, puzzling.

He shrugged. 'I found an interested party, and it looks like we might be able to sell this app for a profit.'

'You did?'

'A few tweaks here, a few tweaks there, and voila. The proceeds, of course, will go to the department.'

'No fair!' said the others.

He raised a hand. 'I know, I know. But the university's board has spoken. There are laws about this and we don't want to cross them.' He turned to Felly. 'However, I had a nice chat with our dean, and Dr Ernie agrees to us having a class outing out of some of the proceeds.'

Felly was delighted. 'Fantastic news. But where to?'

He cracked a smile and shot her a sidewise glance. 'Den Bosch, of course.'

8

Not everyone from Felly and Pascal's university course joined the excursion to Den Bosch. Their train fare was covered by the department's limited extra curricular budget. And so was the hotel expense for staff, but students were encouraged to stay in a hostel. Reinier Nolten lived with family in Den Bosch when not in school. So, for him, a weekend home wasn't special. It was the friends he'd bonded with through the capstone project that had made it so, particularly since all had gone so well with the programming and launch of the *Whodunit!* app.

Felly was riding in a front coupé with Kieran and Femke, who'd happily joined in on the mini-vacation from home. Pascal was seated across the aisle, but now leaning in and speaking with some reservation about his upcoming visit with the van de Meervenne family. They had graciously sent a handwritten letter, inviting him for tea after Evi's memorial service. But he confessed to them, 'I'm oddly nervous about meeting these people. I know nothing about my birthmother's family.'

'That's understandable,' said Felly. 'I've always thought Evi Anneveldt a bit of a wild card. I wonder if they're anything like her.'

His smile waxed and waned. 'It's hard wrapping my mind around her really being 'mother', her of all people.' He sighed. 'So, I Googled the house, which on the map appears to be one of those dilapidated mansions in the older section of town.'

Kieran piped in. 'Old money then? Must be nice.'

Felly clicked her tongue. 'Coming from old money doesn't always mean that you still have it.'

'I think it's amazin', like winning the Lotto.'

'Maybe you can retire early now, Pascal,' she said. 'Wouldn't that be great?'

Kieran agreed. 'If wishes were horses.'

Femke was snuggled against her mother, playing on her iPad. 'Wishes aren't horses, Papa.'

The young assistant professor studied the blue-eyed child. 'And do you have a horse, Femke?'

She stared across the aisle at him, nodding her head up and down, her parents shaking their heads, no.

'Ja, ja. Sinterklaas gave him to me.'

'Oh, that horse,' said Felly, 'your plastic horse.'

'Ja, 'Boomerang'.'

Pascal laughed. 'Boomerang?'

With the ease of thumb and index finger, she swiped the iPad's screen and showed him the brand-named Paint Horse that was also involved in an online child's game.

'Oh, I see. A spotted horse. Do you interact with him online too?'

'In case you're wondering,' interrupted Felly, 'we do use child-guards. Femke's quite good at navigating her way through these games too. Aren't you, poppie?'

The child agreed, unabashedly.

He smirked. 'We could have used your skills in our project.'

'It's amazin' how these little ones are so dextrous with the internet. I soon won't be able to keep up with her.'

Felly agreed with her husband. 'Femke's already past my AI skill level.'

'No doubt mine too,' said Pascal. So, what does Boomerang do? Does he go on wild adventures?'

'He chases 'criminoes'.'

'Criminoes? Hmm, he sounds like a brave horse.'

'Mama, do you have juice?' She was clearly done with the man. Pascal didn't appear fased but merely smiled and sat back in his seat, gazing out the window and checking text messages then glimpsing the NS app to see when the train would arrive at their destination.

The 's-Hertogenbosch station is run by the NS, or National Dutch Rail System, its modern infrastructure making it possible for electric powered trains since the post-war 1950s. Previous engines were diesel fuelled. The first of the stations, built in the late 19th century, was constructed to be easily dismantled with minimal waste if the then fortified city were ever under attack. This was later replaced by brick and the tracks realigned to fit in with its relocation south of the original. The station caught fire in the Second World War with bits and pieces of the original included in its later reconstruction. A more modern design was erected in the late 20th century that included an extended roof and aerial walkway, though the Dutch windy weather does not make it a comfortable station to do anything other than check in and out with maybe a quick coffee and snack in-between. So, when their train arrived, the university students said a quick farewell then left to find a hostel, or low-budget hotel, to spend the night in before they went on to explore the city. With his backpack across his shoulder, Reinier appeared with Minke. They chatted briefly with their professors before heading home, Reinier's parents having agreed to let Minke stay the weekend. As for Pascal van Houten, he along with the McNeelas had decided once again to stay at the Golden Tulip's Hotel Central. On their way there they stopped to view the area where Evi, now known to Pascal as his mother, had drowned. Their steps made crunching sounds on the mid-December grasses, still green but frozen, as they walked along the knoll.

Felly directed Kieran to the water's edge by the bridge. 'This is where Evi drowned,' she said. 'Or at least where she'd been found floating in the water.'

He eyed the cold cement embankment. 'Such a sad thing to have died this way.'

'Well, I'll part company with you here,' said Pascal. 'I'm off to give my condolences.'

Kieran shook his hand. 'Best of luck, mate.'

Felly said, 'Would you like to meet up with us again for dinner? Or do you think you'll still be with the van de Meervennes?'

'No, it's just a tea. And, yes, let's do that. I'll text when I'm able to, then we can decide where to meet up.'

'Poor fella,' said Kieran, watching him depart as little Femke waited patiently by their sides. He then turned to her. 'Well, poppie, I hear there's an ice rink in town.'

It was winter festival and the town of Den Bosch was decorated with festive lights for the holidays.

'Papa wants to take you ice skating? Lucky you!' Felly looked back, glimpsing the knoll. 'I have an idea. Why don't you two check it out while I check us all in? I can meet you at the rink afterwards.'

He turned to Femke. 'Sound like a plan?'

'Papa, papa.' She was jumping up and down now. 'I want to go ice skating.'

Felly laughed. 'I think she's excited.'

'Just a mite.'

'It shouldn't be too hard to find you later, not in a small town like this.'

'Doei, doe, Mama, bye-bye.' Femke was now tugging her father's arm.

'Bye, dag dag,' said her mother.

The two left hand-in-hand as Felly returned to scanning the landscape. She bent down and ran her fingers across the frosted blades of grass, slightly cold and stinging to the touch. It was oh so quiet. Boats wouldn't be travelling the canals much this time of year. And, in the near distance, she heard only the odd one or two muffled vehicular sounds of car tires and motorcycle engines. A few crows landed close by. They were pecking the ground as she moved closer, shooing off the one pecking at a small shiny object. 'What do we have here?' She glimpsed the crows still within close range, brazen and unafraid. 'If only you could talk. What would you have seen? You could tell me if Evi was with someone that night.'

She picked up the plastic bead and rolled it around in the palm of her hand. Her thoughts shifted to Trudi Langmeijer, Dr Vos's secretary. And just how close were the two of them? Business mixing with pleasure? Could they have somehow been involved? But why? She could think of no foreseeable motive, pocketing the bead in her jacket and walking toward the hotel in town. At the front desk, the clerk recognised her from before, smiling. 'Another conference?'

'Hardly,' she said. 'Once a year is plenty. But your hotel is quite lovely.'

'We're glad to have you back. And I see you've booked a suite with futon.'

'For our five-year-old, yes.'

The clerk smiled, handing her a room card. 'I'm sure you'll all be comfortable.'

After depositing her luggage, she left for the main square of stalls displaying various seasonal ornaments and treats for the holidays. Felly bought a mugful of hot spiced wine before heading over to the covered rink the vendor had pointed her toward. She sipped her wine and stood watching Kieran with Femke on rented skates after spotting them undetected. She also saw that her husband had rented what looked like a plastic penguin on flat skis. Handles protruded out of each side of its head, which Femke held onto while being gently pushed across the slick surface. Ingenious, she thought. It reminded her of training wheels on ice. Her little family turned the corner, caught sight of her and waved. She waved back, but Femke let go and fell, causing Kieran to also topple to the side of her. They were both laughing and dusting off ice as they approached the wooden railing.

Felly handed Kieran her mug for a sip. 'Are you all right?' He slugged the rest of it down.

'Whoa, I'm survivin'. But great fun, great fun. Right, poppie. And yer alright, yerself, then?'

The little girl nodded, standing somewhat awkwardly with heels turned in on rented skates. 'Can I have some hot chocolate, Mama?'

Felly glimpsed the wooden enclosure. 'I don't see where you can get any here.'

'I'll just need to turn in all this gear. Take yer skates off, poppie, and we'll search for some together. I wouldn't mind more of that spiced wine, myself.'

Outside was actually warmer than in the rink. And it didn't take long to find a booth that was selling hot chocolate along with slices of holiday stollen, which was a sugared bread dotted with raisins and filled with almond paste. They found another booth and bought more mulled wine then sat on a bench to eat and drink.

'Look at this, Kier.' Felly pulled out the shiny bead from her jacket pocket. 'I found this by the bridge.'

'Like from my LOL bracelet,' said Femke.

'LOL bracelet?'

Felly grinned. 'She thinks it looks like a bead from her child's jewellery-making kit. But this I found when a crow was pecking on it.'

'And how much of this wine have you already had, darlin'?'

'It just so happens that De Vos's secretary has a stress reducing hobby of making these beaded eyeglass chains. And Jolanda, our department secretary, has – or had - one too. She broke hers the other day. I think they're kind of fragile. Anyway, do you think this could have possibly come from one given to Evi too?'

'So, where did ye find this, exactly?'

'Over by the bridge. I found it after you left.'

'By where Evi drowned?'

'Yes...yes!' she said, excitedly.

'Well, that's something, but finding a plastic bead does not a murder make.'

'It could be a clue, though.'

'Hm, maybe. But a flimsy one, at best.'

She rolled it again in her palm, rolling it round and round, thinking out loud. 'A piece to what's been puzzling me all along.'

'Which is what?'

'This Evi, Baas and Trudi triangle.'

'Careful, darlin'. Assumptions without the facts to back them could be dangerous.'

'Indeed, they could. Indeed, they could.' She was still rolling the bead in her hand.

After returning to the hotel, Felly texted Pascal about meeting them for dinner. He replied to count him in and was currently sitting on a café terrace, beer in hand, soaking up the last of the late autumn sun. The memorial service had gone well, and he'd also seen Dr Ernie and his wife, who were paying their respects. 'Along with Baas and Trudi,' he texted. Neither couple had stayed long. Pascal waved them off as they hailed a cab. He got to ride with the van de Meervennes in their limo. 'And I was right,' he wrote her. 'They do live in a dilapidated mansion.' He added how gracious they were to him, apologising even for how it had taken the tragedy of their daughter's death to come into contact with her son. 'Our grandson,' they had added. 'It was a tear-jerk moment for me. Oh, and the maid served us tea in their sitting room. Posh, right? I could get used to this.'

Felly texted back that she was happy to hear all went well. Dinner thoughts included a possible restaurant not far from the Jheronimus Bosch art museum, where she'd had the tasty Indonesian meal before the conference. He agreed that Indonesian sounded good. And she signed off, texting: 'Enjoy your beer. Till soon!'

Kieran was flopped on the bed, shoes off and watching TV sports. Femke was perched on the small futon close by, her attention wrapped up in a Free Spirit Horse adventure game. 'You're going to wear out that iPad,' Felly quipped as she showed Kieran the text.

'Nice,' he said as he read. 'Out of tragedy comes some happiness.'

'I'd say you were right about old money. Pascal could possibly be financially set for life, as there was no talk of other siblings. Oh, and I forgot to ask if they'd shown him any of his mother's personal effects.'

'You mean like what she had on her when she died?'

She nodded her head. 'It didn't seem appropriate to text this right after the funeral. I can ask him later. Oh, and could you make a reservation for four at the Restaurant Bandung? Here, just use my phone. I want to take a shower first.'

He raised his head from the pillow he'd been resting on. 'Any particular time?'

'I don't think Pascal is all that particular. Neither am I. So, you choose. Just order a rice table. And don't make it too late for Femmie.'

He glimpsed his daughter tapping away on her iPad, thinking she didn't look too particular either. 'Okay, then sixish it is.'

Femke locked onto his gaze and shot back a smile. 'What's a rice table, Papa?'

'A table made of rice, of course,' he said.

Felly caught sight of his still boyish grin after all these years. Charmingly devilish. 'What are you telling her now, Kier?'

Femke beamed over at her mother. 'We're gonna eat a rice table.'

The restaurant was a good fifteen-minute walk from the hotel, the air brisk with sun poking through clouds that had suddenly appeared. Dutch fall weather was often fickle. 'As fickle as a weathercock,' said Felly. But it wasn't an unpleasant walk, though they did have to bundle up with coats, scarves and mittens, which only Felly seemed to be wearing. Femke kept losing her mittens and scarves, and Kieran didn't bother.

The corner restaurant was a block east of the river canal. And they entered to the sound of tinkling bells, which Felly thought quaint on her first visit. To her they added to the charm of a local haunt. Drinks were ordered when menus were supplied, and they tried not to salivate when looking over photos of sauteed meats, crisp vegetables steamed with coconut sauce, spring rolls and rice topped with crispy coconut shavings.

Being occupied with menu choices, they hadn't noticed the patron approaching their table and looked up in surprise. 'Well, hello again, Reiner,' said Felly. 'I should have guessed you might be dining here with your family, especially since you're the one who recommended this place to me.'

He smiled and motioned toward Minke, who was looking relaxed in a pink cashmere sweater that had replaced the pinstriped jacket she wore to school. Minke gave a short wave when seeing them looking her way. 'The girl sitting next to Minke, is my bossy little sister, Rinske,' he chortled. 'And, of course, those are my parents, Dirk and Jenny.'

Felly rose from her chair and followed him over to his table, introducing herself as one of Reinier and Minke's professors. Both parents shook her extended hand while Minke sat grinning. Then Felly motioned to her husband

and daughter, who returned the smiles as well. 'Pascal's joining us too,' she said to the parents; 'He's been working with us on the course capstone project.' They gave her approving nods. Then she left them to finish their meals and returned to her own seat. They continued to stare, so she raised her wine glass to them before turning back to Kieran with raised brow. 'Okay then, have we decided on what looks good?'

'Everything,' he replied.

She glimpsed the menu card. 'Do you suppose Pascal is vegetarian? I didn't think to ask.'

Just then her colleague entered the establishment and rubbed his hands together. His jacket and scarf he had left hanging on a peg in the hall with the tinkling bells. 'It's turning nippy outside. So, hey, everyone. It smells great in here, doesn't it?' He pulled out a chair as Felly directed him to the other table. Everyone smiled and waved. Reinier's father, however, looked like he'd just swallowed fermented seaweed.

'That's an odd reaction,' she said, eyeing the man sidewise as she sipped her wine.

Kieran had been eyeing the family too. 'Yer man over there, ye mean? I caught that too.'

'Wonder what's up with him?'

'Who the bleedin' knows?' he said dismissively. 'So, Pascal. Ye've had a spot of news then?'

Pascal was seated with his back to the other table and hadn't noticed anything untoward, not even when the others quickly finished their dinner and left without a farewell. 'Yes,' he said. 'I couldn't have asked for a better outcome. Beer, please,' he told the approaching waiter. 'They gave me a few of my mother's things, some childhood photos, her class ring. Oh, and the things from the police station when I enquired about them.'

'Good,' said Felly. 'Anything interesting?'

He smiled. 'The photos, yes.'

She flustered. 'Yes, of course.'

He handed her the Ziplock bag he was carrying. 'All that's here is a well-worn wallet and reading glasses. Come to think of it, her iPhone might clue us into the last person she talked to...unless it's password protected. Just a thought, but I'm sure the police would've already checked those messages anyway.'

'Glasses, you say?'

'Her reading glasses.' He reached into the bag and showed them to her more clearly, gold-rimmed and linked with a broken chain, a beaded chain.

Felly caught her breath. 'After you left, I found a bead similar to these on the ground by the bridge.' She fingered the broken chain while drawing the plastic bead from her pocket. 'A match,' she said. 'See, a match.'

'It looks like it belongs, yes.' He eyed her, puzzling. 'But what does it mean?'

'It means that it's time we talk to Trudi.'

'Oh, right. She makes these. Oh, Felly, surely you don't think...?'

'I'm not thinking anything, not until we talk to her.'

He let out his breath. 'But what possible motive...?'

She shrugged her shoulders. 'It wouldn't hurt to ask if the two had, for whatever reason, met before the conference.'

'No, it wouldn't at that. So, it's been a long day and I'm famished. Have you guys ordered yet?'

Femke, who'd remained quiet all this time, spoke suddenly. 'We're eating rice tables!'

'Rice tables, eh? Well, I'm so hungry I could eat a horse.'

Femke eyed him with horror, clutching the plastic horse she'd brought with her to her chest.

He laughed. 'Not Boomerang, of course!'

Pascal checked out the following morning. While at the front desk, he sighted Felly and Kieran in the dining area. He went over to them, backpack slung over his shoulder. 'I have some things I still have to do at school. So, I'm heading home early.'

Felly was buttering her daughter's toast, Kieran drinking coffee while murdering breakfast eggs over two slices of ham. 'Sorry to hear that. You could have joined us. We're going to do a bit more city exploring today.'

'Sounds nice, but I've been putting off compiling end of semester marks, which I need to turn in before winter break.'

'Calculating grades, what a thankless task.'

'I know. Have you turned yours in yet?'

'I always do mine as soon as I can. Why prolong the pain of paperwork? Do you want grape or strawberry jam, poppie?'

Femke pointed to the strawberry packet, engrossed in her meal. 'Well, Pascal, it's been a pleasure working on the serious gaming project with you.'

'The pleasure's all mine.'

Kieran reached over and briefly shook the other man's hand. 'Safe travels. Felly wants us to go have a look at the Jheronimus Bosch Art Center. So, we're staying the extra day.'

111

'I still need to go there.'

'You haven't been yet?' Felly looked surprised. 'I thought you'd at least want to see the 500-year-old astronomical clock. It's hilarious, though frightening, I'm sure, to all those superstitiously religious 16th century townsfolk.'

'Customs and cultures,' said Pascal with a grin. 'They do trip us up sometimes.'

Kieran asked. 'Have you always wanted to be an anthropologist then?'

'Cultural anthropologist,' he corrected. 'Two different things. I've never been keen on digging up bones, but social structures have always interested me.'

'Me too...linguistically speaking,' said Felly.

He turned back to her husband. 'How about you, Kieran? Always the legal eagle?'

The other man laughed at the term, shaking his head, no. 'I was in the Irish Garda for several years.'

'I would never have guessed that, not in a millennium.'

'And why not?'

'I guess I'm guilty of stereotyping, but I'm thinking ramrod straight, and linear in thought. That's my version of the typical police I've encountered, which is definitely not you. So, why the switch from cop to counsellor? Did Felly have something to do with it?'

Kieran chortled. 'She always has something to do with it.'

'Don't let him fool you,' she quipped. 'He's just being modest. Kieran already had a bachelors in criminal law when we met. And, he being an inspector, well, I thought him more detective than your average guard.'

'I confess I started out in medicine, myself. For a brief time, I wanted to be a chemist.'

'Interesting paths we choose to follow. Felly's twin is into corporate law.'

Pascal blinked. 'A twin, you say?'

'My twin brother, yes. And two entirely different entities.'

'I wouldn't be so sure about that,' he teased. 'I imagine you'd be a good lawyer. You seem to have a built-in bullshit detector.'

'Believe me, I'm easily misled.'

'Ha! That makes two of us. Well, this has been fun, but I better take off before I miss my train. I'm sure we'll bump into each other again before the holidays. If not, have a good one.'

'We still need to have that chat with Trudi, remember?'

'Yes, but no rush. It might be best to wait until next term, when we're all back together again.'

As they watched Pascal exit the hotel's revolving doors, Kieran warned, 'Just be careful when ye speak with that department secretary. Accusing someone of a crime can be libellous...even dangerous, especially if they're actually guilty of something.'

'No worries. It'll just be a chat, not a confrontation.'

'Okay, good.' He rose, yawning and stretching. 'Are we done here? I'm up for an adventure to the hilarious art centre.'

Felly turned to their daughter. 'Finished, poppie?'

'Strouberries are so yummy.'

'I can see that by what you're wearing on your face. Here, use this napkin.'

The child took the table linen and wiped all around her mouth as Felly told Kieran, 'The 'Garden of Earthly Delights' is quite the tryptich. It even puts the red-light district to shame.'

He raised a brow. 'Not safe for the little one's eyes then?'

'Oh, it's quite safe. She won't have a clue about all those medieval themes of good and evil. Most likely Femke will just fixate on the strawberries, anyway. The giant one, in particular.'

He laughed at the image conjured in his mind. 'Yes, what does a child know about such things?'

9

With marks turned in and the term winding down, everyone began discussing winter vacations, some planning skiing trips to the French Alps, others escaping to the warmth of Spain in time-shared villas. Felly and Kieran's thoughts turned to Ireland, though her parents objected to them leaving before Christmas Eve. Anneke had insisted, and they relented, to take an Aer Lingus flight to visit Kieran's family on Christmas morning. It had been the van Vliet tradition to have children and spouses, and now grandchild, attend mass with them at the Hartebrugkerk, the church of the bridge of hearts, where Felly and Kieran had married six years ago.

The Hartebrugkerk, known to the locals as the *Porta Coeli*, or 'Heaven's Gate', was constructed in a classicist style and not too ornate for one built in 1836, a romantic era with angels and cupids added in the mix. This was built in the constrained manner of the Dutch, its walls plastered white and its interior ceiling vaulted. There were two alcoves dedicated to the statue of Christ's mother, Mary, that bathed her in candlelight. Stone reliefs also adorned the side walls below arching stained glass windows, and these displayed the stations of the cross along with statues on pedestals of various saints. Saint Anthony was a clear favourite, featured in wood in the wings and also outside in a stone relief as an ex-voto, appearing to be blessing a dog with the Dutch inscription, 'What love can accomplish'.

The church was well-known for its love of animals, which was even discussed in their newsletter that featured an abbey in Maastricht where Trappist monks took care of Livar pigs, a breed of pigs from Limburg.

Holiday work parties were also in the mix. Felly attended Kieran's office party with him, a formal affair at the Amstel Hotel, which was a beautiful setting along the east bank of the river Amstel. For him her visible support was especially important now that he had become the newest partner of the De Veer Law Group. The university faculty celebrations were more informal, the humanities department having decided to meet up at Café Barrera for what the Dutch call a 'borreltje'. There drinks and appetisers were served in rounds, and it was known as one of Leiden's popular local hangouts along the Rapenburg canal, which was within cycling distance from campus. Kieran would stay home, though, watching Femke as the borrel was staff only with the department once again footing the bill on its small extracurricular budget.

'You won't be too disappointed, will you, Kier?' They were sitting together on the couch, Kieran engrossed in the All-Ireland football final.

'Go have some craic, darlin'. Missin' a borrel is nothing that's gettin' me excited right now. I'm on the edge of my seat here, thinking it's time we beat them Dubs.'

'Beat dem Dubs,' mimicked the five-year-old. She was seated on his other side and holding both cats who were flopped in her arms, their eyes darting around for an escape route.

'I hear the Dublin players are a pretty fierce bunch.'

Kieran turned to his daughter. 'Did ye hear that, poppie? Sacrilege!'

'Yeah, sack-er-lidge.' She bit down on a Dorito chip, the cats now fleeing from her grip.

'Okay, I'm off. Have fun you two. Don't eat too many of those chips, Femke. They bother your tummy.'

'I won't, Mama,' she said, popping another in her mouth.

It was another day of late autumn sun and Felly felt lucky with the weather, though it still wasn't warm enough to be out long without a coat and sweater. She wore both, including the scarf she wrapped around her neck before hopping on her bike. The corner café was one where she and Kieran had spent a lot of time, its location convenient and surroundings overlooking a quaint footbridge across the canal. Above the café was a student house, its balcony bearing the sign 'Welgelen', or well-situated, where scenes from 'The Soldier of Orange' had been filmed. She glimpsed the upper deck at her approach and waved to Reinier when catching sight of him among the group. Students were always up to something, as they were that afternoon, dressed in ugly Christmas sweaters as they hung off the wrought iron balcony with white-painted wood trim. Beers in one hand and dextrously checking their phones in the other, they appeared oblivious to the rest of the world, their unsightly sweaters sharing their private joke to the world, their world of academia and not yet subjected to the outside workforce. Temporary student housing could often accommodate a half dozen youth at a time, as not many minded roughing it for a bit of comradery. And this afternoon they were just having a laugh together before going their separate ways, heading home on winter break.

After chaining her bicycle to a side lamp post, Felly stepped through ebony doors and recognised colleagues sitting and standing around an elongated bar. She was looking forward to the holidays, relieved that the somewhat stressful term was over. On a whim, she ordered the holiday special, a pink gin and tonic served with raspberries on ice. The smiling bartender served her the pretty cocktail, which he set down among several shades of beer, wine and whiskey that were sitting half-full atop Heineken coasters. The music was loud, so loud she could hardly hear herself think, which to her didn't matter much. What was there to think about during the next month's reprieve but what to eat and who to share it with? And the festive mood was contagious, the sea of voices chattering away about nothing in particular. She saw Reinier again. He had come down and was talking to Pascal, looking rather apologetic, she observed. Pascal didn't seem all that pleased, either.

She went over to them just as Reinier turned and walked off. 'Everything good? Trouble with grades?'

'No, nothing like that,' said Pascal. 'Reinier just informed me that he's leaving us for Erasmus spring term.'

'Really? He looked to be having so much fun with his mates a few moments ago. So, why Erasmus?'

'It's his father's doing, I'm afraid, with the excuse that he wants him closer to home.'

She frowned. 'Leiden's not all that far from Rotterdam. I fail to see the difference. Such a pity. I'm sad to lose him. He's such a fun student to have. Creative, energetic. He did so well in my course too.'

Pascal lifted his whiskey glass and eyed the warm amber, no comment.

'I wonder how Minke's taking it. I thought they were a couple now?'

'It's my fault, Felly.'

'What? Why would it be your fault?'

'I knew his father looked familiar when I caught sight of him at the Indonesian restaurant.'

She listened, her drink in hand now bringing it to her lips and tasting the pleasant mixture. She drank more, waiting for him to continue.

'This isn't easy for me to say, but I knew Dirk when I was younger. I mean, I knew him long before my partner and I were together.'

'What? What are you telling me?'

'Don't get me wrong. I was no older than Reinier, and it had been a one-night stand.'

'You don't mean...? But he's a family man.'

'It doesn't matter. It should, but it often doesn't with guys like him.'

'You mean guys like him who goes both ways?'

He nodded his head. 'And I guess, to him, the wife doesn't have to know. It's none of my business, anyway.'

She was speechless before finding her voice again. 'Why doesn't the wife have to know? I would think that, of all people, she should.'

'Of course, she should. But I'm not that guy.'

'No, you most certainly aren't. And never in a million years would I have put the two of you together.'

He snorted. 'Well, in my world it doesn't work like that. I'm going to get another drink. Do you want a top-up?'

'I'm good. I'm still nursing this one.'

'What is that you're drinking, anyway?' he laughed. 'I saw it advertised next to a lit-up plastic snowman.'

'It's a pink gin and tonic with raspberries, their holiday special. It's quite good, actually. Cherry flavoured.'

'Cherry and raspberries? I think I'll pass. Be back in a tick.'

She scanned the crowded room when a wait-person came up to her. She was bearing a large round serving tray full of shrimp and salmon slices atop baguettes that looked to be smeared with cream cheese and herbs. 'Een hapje?' asked the woman.

'O, lekker, dank je wel.' She took one.

'Alsje,' a shortened version of 'you're welcome'.

Felly bit into the hors d'oeuvre as the server melted back into the crowd and made a beeline for Dean Huijsman, a few warm bodies away. He was well-known by all the students there, and the server was probably one of them. He took a salmon slice, looking over to Felly and smiling. She, in turn, raised her glass, seeing him losing no momentum while chatting away with another colleague Felly thought familiar but didn't really recognise. His secretary, Jolanda Wiersma, left their company and came over to her. 'What are you doing sitting at the bar all by your lonesome? Come join our group. You know, Saskia, right? She's fairly new to the department.'

'I've never had the pleasure. What does she teach?'

'Women's studies. Want me to introduce you?'

'Maybe later, thanks. Pascal is with me now. He's just refreshing his drink. And how are you? Enjoying the semester finally being over?'

'Oh yes. You?' She nodded her head about to speak, but Jolanda went on. 'The conversation at our table is boring, anyway. Everyone's bragging about their upcoming ski trips. Oh, to be paid a professor's salary.'

Felly laughed out loud. 'I don't know which professors you're talking about. I certainly don't get paid anything to brag about. Then again, I'm only working part-time these days.'

'Who needs money when you've got that handsome hunk of a lawyer to come home to?'

She laughed even harder. 'What are you drinking, Jolanda?'

The dark-eyed woman sidled closer. 'Shh, I'm on my third vodka. Slides down easy, if you know what I mean.'

'So, are you doing anything special for Christmas?'

'I'm taking the night train to Berlin and spending a few days there with my ex.'

'I've never been to Berlin, myself. The airport, yes, once. But I never count airport stopovers.'

'No, not much to see in an airport. Berlin is a vibrant city full of museums. And my ex is fun. I just couldn't live with him. He's one of those kooky artists...paints industrial art. Not to my taste.' She shrugged her shoulders, nursing her glass. 'He manages a nice income out of it, though. Yet, he lives like a bohemian. His choice, not mine. Thus, the split.'

'Sounds like an interesting person to know.'

'Oh, he is that. We've always been good friends. As I said, I just couldn't live with the guy.'

'I know plenty that.' She eyed the returning Pascal, smiling.

'Hello, Jolanda,' he greeted. 'Ah, vacation time, yes? I'm going skiing, myself. You?'

'What did I tell you,' laughed Jolanda. 'Everyone's going skiing...but me.'

'Well, I'm not,' said Felly. 'We're having Christmas Eve dinner with the parents. Then we're heading over to

Ireland to spend the rest of the holiday with Kieran's family. Femke loves them so.'

'Your little one's such a doll,' cooed the department secretary. 'Don't you think so, Pascal?'

He grinned at the women sidewise. 'A little stinker, all right.'

'Oh, there's Trudi. Well, I'm going to leave the two of you to discuss your skiing, which must be grand in Ireland with all those lovely hills and valleys.' Before Felly could respond, she gasped, saying, 'And there she goes again. I'd better catch her before she slips away. I've been learning how to make her elegant eyeglass chains, but I still need more pointers.' And she spun away before they could say goodbye.

'Jolanda's something else.'

'A whirlwind,' laughed Felly.

Pascal nodded in agreement. 'So, back to the painful subject of Dirk Nolten.'

'Pascal, you don't need to explain yourself to me. I'm okay, really. What you do is your own affair.'

'No, I want to explain myself. Reinier's your student too, after all.'

'And does he know about his father? About his proclivities? Is that what you were discussing when I came over. I'm sorry if I interrupted you.'

'You didn't interrupt us. And, no, I don't think Reinier does know. He was only upset that his father was pulling him out of school here...away from all his mates. He doesn't particularly want to go to Erasmus. He doesn't know anyone there.'

'Well, then why should he?'

'Because his father's got him over an economic barrel. He refuses to support him if he doesn't.'

She pursed her lips. 'What an ....'

'Yes...but more like running scared.'

'And under the guise of wanting him to be closer to home.'

'It could be legit, Felly...his parents wanting him to attend university closer to home. I know that especially the younger students are enjoying their new-found freedom, but it can get expensive if the parents are in higher income brackets that don't qualify for much government funding.'

'The father's being deceitful about his motives,' she reiterated. 'So, what was going on between you and him, anyway? I mean, if you don't mind sharing. Please tell me if you don't. You won't hurt my feelings.'

She noticed the flush in his cheeks when he brought his whiskey glass to his mouth just then and drank it down. 'I don't suppose you've heard of the Blue River Sauna?'

'The, what?' She shook her head, no. 'Is that here in Leiden?'

'The Hague, and it's where we met and had a fling...a short fling when I was about Reinier's age, as I said. How old was I? I don't know, around nineteen?'

'Wow, you must have left some kind of impression on him if he still remembers you from ten years ago.'

'I'd honestly forgot, myself. So, I was surprised when he phoned last night. We spoke for about an hour. He's not a bad man, really, just still somewhat confused.'

'I don't agree with you. He's being dishonest, both to himself and those others he now has close to him, who trust him. If he's bisexual he should come out and talk about it with them. Don't you think? That's what I think.'

'Which you think because you're not bisexual. It's harder to do so than you could imagine. I'm not bisexual, myself, though I do appreciate female beauty. Well, like yours. You're a beautiful woman, Felly. I've always enjoyed your company too.'

'Why, thank you, Pascal. Likewise. I'm just so sad to be hearing this about Reinier, though. How it must make you feel as well. Are you all right then?'

He shrugged. 'Nothing I can do about it. It's just one of those things.'

'Yes, she parroted. 'Just one of those things.'

Kieran had tried his hand at making dinner for Felly and Femke before she returned, the pleasant odours of fried sausage and potatoes permeating the houseboat and accosting the senses. 'You smell like people,' he spoke as he turned around, kitchen apron on and spatula in hand. Then he kissed her lips, but she was laughing.

'I want to get a picture of this and put it on Facebook, entitled: Kieran in the kitchen, a changeling?' She laughed even harder thinking about actually doing it, but she wouldn't.

'Very funny. And how was the borrel?'

'Interesting as well. So, you can actually cook something other than pancakes?'

'For all that it's worth. I had to do something. Our poppie was hungry.'

Just then one of the cats darted out of the back hall. Ears flat and eyes bulging, it sprang atop the grey couch, puffing up its fur and attacking one of the blue embroidered throw pillows. 'What are you doing, Puk?' Felly gasped. 'It's a wonder we have any house left with these silly cats.'

'That's not the half of it. So, I'm setting a plate for you on the kitchen table. Femmie and I have already eaten.'

She sat down and took in the somewhat dishevelled living space, a plush bear here, a plastic horse and doll there, pieces of a *Candy Land* board game sprawled across the dining room floor. 'You've been busy entertaining yourselves as well. Where is our little darling?'

'I don't know. She's been awfully quiet. Nice, eh? Silence is bliss.'

She nodded her head, digging into her meal. 'My ears are still ringing from the deafening noise at the café.'

'Fun afternoon then?'

'Mmhm.' She forked a sausage and potato, putting them in her mouth and chewing. 'And you keep telling me you can't cook. This isn't bad at all. But, yes, lots of partying students – and professors – before dispersing for home.'

'Well, I for one am ready for the holidays. Ma belled up at half five, over the moon to see her granddaughter again. Ye wouldn't believe the stack of presents she's got waitin' for her, waitin' to spoil the child.'

She forked another piece of sausage. 'Bridget's a sweetheart. It'll be nice seeing her again too. Speaking of calls.' And she told Kieran about Pascal's phone conversations with Reinier father, who had also suddenly decided to have his son study elsewhere.

He whistled, long and slow, saying, 'Sins of the fathers.'

'Sins of the fathers?' she puzzled.

He nodded his head. 'Playing catch up with the actions ye have to account for. I never got that biblical saying until I was in the force. It was then I saw clear as a bell how life has a domino effect. There's no escaping choices and outcomes.'

'I'm just sad for Reinier. It's often the innocent ones whose lives are affected by these choices and outcomes

125

you mention. And the wife? Jeez, do you think she does know? About her husband, I mean?'

Kieran shrugged his shoulders.

'But how could she not? Maybe she does know and just lives with it. Erasmus is a good school, anyway. I hear they've got a great financial department. And Reinier will do fine. But I'm sure it's heartbreaking for Minke.'

'Have you spoken with your students, yourself?'

She shook her head, no. 'Pascal just told me this afternoon at the café. Heartbreaking, isn't it?'

'It is that. So, there's more sausage and potatoes in the pan.'

'I'm good, thanks. Tasty and satisfying, foodwise. Thanks for leaving me some.' She shot him a smile that made him forget any washing up. Then she sighed. 'I suppose we should check on our little ragamuffin.'

He followed her in back and peeked into Femke's room. 'Whatcha doing, poppie?'

It was now understandable why Puk had made a mad dash for the living room. Flopped atop the little girl's lap was the other cat, and it was wearing the curly red and black wig of Saint Nicholas's helper, the black Pete. She looked up at them, all smiles with teacup in hand. 'Want a cuppah?'

They both laughed out loud.

'Well, do you?' she asked with indignance.

Kieran smiled back lovingly, first at his daughter and then her mother. 'A spot of tea would be grand.'

10

Felly cycled to the university's humanities department on Monday to return the few books she had borrowed for a semester course she had been teaching. While still in the hallway, she heard a female voice from inside the offices chanting something like 'Ooohmmmh', and it was coming from Dr De Vos's office. She entered and peeked in, surprised to see the secretary, Trudi Langmeijer, in a meditative pose while stringing what looked like glass pearls to a silver-tone chain. Should she interrupt the woman? She hesitated, knowing this was her chance to ask about the piece she had found by the bridge in Den Bosch. Yet, how would she go about enquiring about such a thing without sounding rude and intrusive? She went over to the coffee maker by the now vacated desk of Jolanda Wiersma, the department secretary whom Felly guessed was already visiting the artistic ex after taking a night train to Berlin. She poured a cup of coffee then smiled in on Trudi. 'Good morning,' she said. 'Not yet left for the holidays?'

The other woman looked up, startled.

Felly pointed at the shiny pearls. 'How lovely. Jolanda told me you were making these. You've been teaching her to make them as well, yes?'

Trudi nodded her head. The chanting had stopped but she continued stringing beads. 'She'd found some nice rubber loop ends to match and was quite pleased with the result.'

'Oh, that reminds me of something I wanted to ask you about.' She pulled out the small bead she'd been carrying around in her jacket. 'I found this in the grass by the bridge in Den Bosch. Some crow was pecking on it. Do you think it could it have possibly belonged to Evi?'

'Let me see.' Trudi took it from her, inspecting the small, round piece of plastic. 'Standard issue. Could have been hers. By the bridge, you say?'

'Yes.'

She squeezed her eyes and lowered her head, ridges of a helmet shape haircut falling before her like a knife. 'And you were just having a walk around? Searching for clues, I gather. You do have that reputation.'

Felly cleared her throat, thinking she wouldn't let this other woman get under her skin. 'On my way back to the station, yes.'

'I hope you realise that this is no kind of evidence. Still, I wouldn't mind holding onto it. Can I? I wouldn't want anyone else getting any ideas.'

'Like the police, you mean?'

'For instance, yes. You never know.'

'So, why worry it you think it's no kind of evidence, as you say?'

Trudi shifted her pose, eyeing the neck strap she'd been stringing. 'Would you like one too...an eyeglass chain? They're also good for sunglasses.'

'Why, thank you.'

'This one's almost ready. Consider it a Christmas gift.'

Felly looked around for a stool and sat down to finish her coffee as she watched Trudi expertly attach crimp beads to the end of beading wires.

'These hold everything together,' the other instructed. 'Otherwise, you'll have excess slippage in the strand, which could spill over onto the jewellery clasp.' She suddenly sighed and rested her hands on her lap. 'I have a confession to make.'

'Oh?' Eyes widening, swallowing hard and praying not to give away any curiosity rush.

'But you'll have to promise me it goes no further.'

'Nothing illegal, I hope.'

She shook her head, no. 'Not that, I swear.'

Felly crossed her heart.

'Seriously,' reiterated Trudi.

'Okay, sorry. What is it then?'

'I was there that evening with Evi.'

The room grew suddenly still. 'You were?'

'Yes, but it's not like what you could possibly be imagining. She and I were old schoolmates, you see. We go way back to middle school. And, on that day, Evi called from where she'd been staying with family in Den Bosch. I could tell she'd been crying when I answered, saying she was desperate to talk to me...but not over the phone. She pleaded with me to come early and meet her in person, meaning the day before everyone was coming for the conference. I didn't even think about it. I immediately packed my bags and took the next train going to Den Bosch.'

'I thought you all told the police you'd carpooled there together.'

'They did...just not me.'

'But...?'

'Yes, they gave me an alibi.' Eyeing her coolly, she went on. 'They are my good friends, my colleagues.' Shifting her position, she smoothed down the loose-fitting patterned pants she was wearing.

'Okay, but why would you need them to alibi you?'

'Why do you think?' she snapped. 'Anyway, that's when Evi told me her dreadful news, the news she'd got that morning about her cancer spreading to her brain and kidneys. She wanted me to go out drinking with her.'

'You went drinking?' Felly was astonished.

'With my old friend who was terminal, yes. What did she have to lose?'

'Well....'

She went on. 'I knew she'd been taking Oxycodone for the pain, and Oxy and alcohol don't mix. But Evi was so distraught, so insistent that we go out drinking. How could I say no to her?' She raised her hands and shrugged. 'Which is also when she dropped the bomb that she was Pascal's birthmother.'

Felly nodded her head. 'He said as much to me.'

'He did? But how could he...?'

'Through a letter the van de Meeveenes sent him.'

'Oh? Well, she'd sworn me to secrecy not to tell him until she'd had the chance to. And he's never said a word to either me or...?'

'Or, who? Dr De Vos?'

When did he receive this letter, Felly?'

'They'd invited him to tea after the memorial service.'

She sighed. 'This must have been an incredible shock for him. I know that Evi had felt she was running against the clock, asking if I would keep mum because she had wanted to meet up with Pascal after the conference. She thought then that she could finally explain everything to him. She had hoped, anyway. She had so many regrets.'

'I'm sure she did. Sadly, she got her wish via her parents. So, where did Evi get the Anneveldt name? Was she married?'

Trudi nodded her head. 'Another sad story, which lasted only a year. Evi was newly wed to an anthropology professor, and she had gone to Nepal with him as he was studying indigenous tribes there. When she returned, she was so excited to share her adventures with everyone, that is, till she found her man in bed with one of his students. She left him immediately, but they were never formally divorced.'

'And where is this husband now?'

'San Francisco, I believe, teaching at Berkeley.' She gestured as if dusting off her hands. 'Good riddance to bad rubbish, poor Evi.'

'That's heartbreakingly sad. Now I'm sorry I wasn't kinder to her.'

The other eyed her keenly. 'I'd never seen you acting untoward.'

'No, not really. But I am guilty of stereotyping.'

'Aren't we all?' chortled Trudi.

'No, I mean it. I'm ashamed to say that I pre-judged her by her appearance.'

'Ah, well, bless. Evi always was the bohemian child.'

'And quite popular with her students.'

'Yes, she was.'

'So, how was it that the two of you were wandering about the Wilhelminabrug in the middle of the night?'

'That's just it, we weren't. We'd been drinking in the pub, just pulling up memories and chatting about life, which was when she told me about Pascal and how she'd wanted to tie up loose ends before she, before she....' She grew suddenly silent, then said, 'I had so many questions.'

Felly sighed. 'I would have too.'

'But we parted company there. And I swear to you that I saw her get into a taxi and ride off toward home. I was waiting on one too, which brought me back to the hotel.'

'You checked in early then?'

'I did. I spent the night in your room, in fact. I just booked it for a night earlier. It was vacant, so why not? And I met everyone else in the morning who were carpooling together.'

Felly rubbed her chin reflexively. 'And Pascal? Was he really in that carpool too?'

'As far as I know. But he didn't look like one who'd just had the shock of his life when I saw him the next morning. It was Baas and I who were red-eyed. And we didn't let on. I didn't want to break Evi's promise.'

'Sounds like you'd shared it with your boss, though.'

Trudi eyed her sheepishly. 'That's different. Baas and I are close, but I swear to you it went no further.'

'Well, I believed Pascal when he told me about the van de Meervennes.'

'I hope you understand, Felly, that if I'd told this to the police.... I mean, what would they have thought?'

'Not much, I guess, especially since the medical report had determined her death as accidental.'

'None of us knew this then, though. The report of Evi's drowning had just happened sometime after midnight.'

132

Felly nodded her head. 'Still, I've always thought it best to come clean with the police. Weren't you worried about obstructing justice?'

'Absolutely not. I'm not guilty and I have nothing to hide.'

'Except the account that maybe you were the last one to see Evi alive.'

'What are you getting at, Felly? Do you think I killed Evi?'

'No, I don't think that now. But something just doesn't sit right about all this,' she confessed. 'So, let's say that Evi had been murdered. Not by you, but by someone else. But who? And why? What could've have been their motive for doing so?'

The other woman sighed, long and hard. 'I have my suspicions, but at the moment that's all they are.'

'But if you suspect someone, when will you know for sure?'

'I want to make some calls and talk to a few people. But, please, keep what I've said just between us.' Her normally aloof eyes took on a pleading look.

'I promise you that I will.' Felly then told her she could keep the little bead she'd found, though she still didn't trust the woman, not a hundred percent. It was certain now that she was holding back something. But what was it?

Trudi thanked her and, in reply, gave her the eyeglass chain she'd been working on. 'All finished. Happy holidays.'

Felly rose from her chair with an appreciative smile. 'You do beautiful work, thank you.'

'You're welcome, and thank you too. It did feel good to get this off my chest.'

As Felly left the building, she thought about how Trudi's colleagues had been alibiing her, thinking how she now understood Pascal's reluctance to confront the woman with her. 'Why hadn't he just said that to me? It would have saved a lot of energy on my part. So many secrets that department has.' She sighed, muttering, 'Birds of a feather,' the phrase as old as the biblical Ecclesiastic proverb. 'Birds of one kind and colour flocking and flying together,' she repeated. 'Birds of one anthropological feather, all right.'

She hopped on her bike and cycled through the late autumn tree-laden neighbourhoods; some foliage still lush as the trees were rooted in the waters of the meandering canals. There were even leaves remaining on certain non-deciduous trees, the linden and poplars, as well as the willows, their leaves turning only yellow and brown. She was ready for winter and looking forward to the family holidays, loving her mother's traditional Christmas Eve dinners of minced lamb and 'stoofpeertjes; pears steamed in red wine, cinnamon sugar and cloves. Then there was the Christmas Day ramshackle Irish family's hodgepodge of turkey, ham or chicken served with stuffing and potatoes. For dessert they usually had an assortment of rum-based puddings and homemade mince pies. Only after all had pleasantly stuffed their faces, would there be a round of gift giving, which was something Felly hadn't been accustomed to growing up. She and her twin were raised to only give gifts on Saint Nicholas Day, the holiday that was mostly for children.

On a whim, Felly made a detour through Evi Anneveldt's neighbourhood, switching gears and pedalling slowly, only pausing when approaching the house. She stopped before it, looking around. Did she detect movement inside? Shadows of trees and other foliage could easily trick one's mind into thinking so. She set down her bike to get a closer look and crept up to a window, peering in. She did see someone there. No doubt about it now. And she thought she recognised a face as she moved in closer to register whose it was. Should she alert the police? But what if this were a relative who had had the right to be there? She would be making a scene by getting involved, embarrassing herself again. But, if this were so, why weren't there any lights? She backed away and phoned Kieran, who instructed her to leave the premises immediately. She promised him she would. Then, right after, she phoned the police. She hopped back on her bike and cycled the block, thinking she should really double-back and wait for the authorities. Yes, this is what she would do. She turned around, watching now from a short distance away where no one would see her. And she waited. It wasn't long before two official cars pulled up to the house and four uniformed officers got out, two approaching the house, the others lingering close by as they scanned the perimeter of the vehicle. One sighted her watching. He waved her over as the others entered the house. She bit down on her lips, knowing that Kieran would be disappointed with her.

'Are you the one reporting the break-in, Felicia McNeela van Vliet, right?' asked the agent at her approach.

'Yes,' she said, 'that's me. I want to add my apologies if it's someone from the family in the house. It's only because there aren't any lights on, that I thought it might be a prowler and you should be notified.'

'You were right in letting us know, thank you. And if you wouldn't mind waiting here, please. I'd like to ask you a few follow-up questions.'

She nodded with mounting apprehension. What had she got herself into?

The officers entering the house lingered for what seemed to Felly an excruciatingly long time, now thinking she'd best phone Kieran so he wouldn't worry. Yet, she wasn't looking forward to doing so. They'd had few tiffs as a couple, but this might turn into one. She called, regardless, his voice not sounding well-pleased. He advised that she answer truthfully any questions posed to her and not add anything else. 'Then, for the love of God, darlin', come the feck home.'

The officer beside her stirred, picking up his radio and speaking into it, eyes peeled on the house. Felly glimpsed toward where he was looking, at the man he was now moving towards who was being brought out in cuffs.

And Dirk Nolten's eyes locked onto hers, he grimaced as she gasped. What the ...? They had recognised each other from their meeting in the restaurant, the Indonesian place in Den Bosch. She shivered with sudden anxiety, thinking she might have just put herself and her family in danger. What had she done?

As the first patrol car drove off, the officer initially addressing Felly had remained to ask a few questions. Heeding Kieran's advice, she briefly answered him that she had been cycling by the house of a recently deceased colleague and noticed activity inside, which was why she had thought it best to alert the police. He thanked her again and detained her no further, though she wasn't looking forward to cycling home and facing Kieran. She knew that his warning not get involved was for her own safety, as he was well aware of her penchant for looking under rocks. *Laat de zaak maar rusten*, as the Dutch say. Just leave things be.

When Felly pulled up to the Rijnkade embankment, she saw only the kitchen light on. And there on the sill were the two Ragdolls who were eyeing her pathetically. She locked up her bike, went in and flipped on more lights. 'Ik ben thuis! I'm home!', she called. No one answered but the mewing cats. They were now rolling around the floor and over her feet. 'You are truly nuisances,' she said, scratching their bellies. They purred instantly. 'It's lucky for you that you're so cute. So, where is everyone, you silly cats?'

She searched the room, and on the countertop, she spied a note propped against a glass next to an open bottle of wine, which she felt was still cold from the fridge. She poured half a glassful and read the note. 'Darling,' it read. 'I've dropped Femke off at Filip and Moira's for the evening. I'm heading over to the police station to see what's what. Maybe I'll be able to find some answers for you then...xoxo.'

She slid onto a barstool and let her bag drop beside her, relieved and curious, relieved mostly that Kieran wasn't upset but was actually attempting to help her. She was curious as to what news he might be able to find. After finishing off her drink, she looked back into the kitchen. No hunger. She decided she'd rather brew up some coffee and wait for his return.

An hour went by and still nothing. Why hadn't Kieran at least texted her? She felt it time to phone Moira, as he probably hadn't told her much of anything when he had dropped off Femke for the sleepover. She knew that Moira would be dying to know all that was going on. Felly convinced herself that she was good at keeping secrets, but who would Moira be telling other than Filip, anyway? Filip, who had trained himself in his profession to be closemouthed about many things. And, other than Felly, Moira's current social circles amounted to those in a local book club that she was involved in. There was also the local green grocer who stocked and sold the fresh jams and curries she made him. Moira was a contented stay-at-home wife who didn't mind watching over her little niece on a whim, as both she and Filip loved Femke as much as they would their own, if they could have had children. No, in her mind, Moira had a pass.

So, the call was not only to pass on information to a trusted old friend who was watching her child, but it was also to kill another hour of wait time. She also felt more relaxed after the call, as their banter ended with enjoyable joking and a lot of laughs. But it wasn't until around midnight that Felly heard a familiar sound of footsteps. She knew that Kieran hadn't eaten that evening and made a sauerkraut and potato casserole with cream sauce on the side. Her appetite remained slight, but the act of cooking had occupied her thoughts and dinner needed only to be warmed up in the microwave. He returned home famished and glad for the hot meal.

She heated up his plate as the tired man sat down and quietly watched. 'An interesting case,' he said as she dished up his plate. He bent his head over the steaming food and breathed in deeply. 'Mm, this all smells delicious.' He took a large bite and washed it down with the bottle of beer she brought him. 'Tastes delicious too.'

'You're killing me with suspense, Kier.'

'Sorry, it's been a long evening. So, I met up with yer man, Dirk, who remembered me from the restaurant. He was defensive, at first, which I'd expected. And he didn't want to have anything a'tal to do with the likes of me, not till I told him that I'm a criminal lawyer and interested in his case. I then asked if he had other legal counsel, and this was when he finally opened up to me.'

'Are you saying you might want to take on his case?"

'Now hear me out, darlin'.' He took another bite followed by a long, satisfying gulp of beer. 'Ye do make a good casserole.'

She reached over the table, kissing his cheek. 'Thank you for pursuing this.'

'I first wanted to get some kind of understanding before offering to take him on, because I wasn't just curious as to why he'd be breaking into that house but also why he'd so quickly embrace my counsel, especially since knowing he's no fan of the woman I'm married to.'

She eyed him with incredulity. 'What does he have against me? I find his son delightful and am only sorry he's leaving us for Erasmus.'

'Because you turned him in, darlin', plain and simple. It's because of you he got arrested.'

'No, it's not. He got arrested because he was breaking and entering Evi's house.'

'Yes, of course he was. But it was you who reported him to the police. If you hadn't been there no one else would've known he was there, either. And he knows that, which is why he's no fan of yours.'

'He's got a lot of nerve,' she said huffily.

'So, it turns out that Dirk is no small chicken. He owns an engineering firm called Nolten Infrastructure and Design, which is big enough to be listed as a corporation instead of sole proprietorship. Have ye heard of it?'

She shook her head, no. 'And why does this matter?'

'It matters because the company has a corporate lawyer in its employ. Dirk's concern is that everything remains as quiet as possible. Bad publicity might harm the firm.'

'I see.' She mulled over what she was hearing from Kieran. 'But why would you want to take on his case? I mean, what's going on with the man?'

'There's a lot going on with him, darlin'. But now that he's taken me on, I'm not at liberty to share much more of it.'

'Oh no...no, no. You can't do this to me.'

'And just what is it that I'm doing?'

'Leaving me hanging like this, Kier.'

'But it's the law.'

'Damn it, damn the law to hell.'

He took another bite of casserole and another swig of beer. 'I feel like that too sometimes. But ye know the law, and we are obliged to follow it.'

She breathed in and out. 'Okay, okay. I'm only asking that you'll keep me abreast of anything you can share with me?'

'Of course, I will, darlin'. And, if it helps, I know how frustratin' this is for ye too.'

'Oh, you don't know the half of it.'

11

With Kieran taken out of the loop, meaning him now legally bound to client-lawyer privilege, Felly reckoned that she was left to her own devices as she attempted to piece together the jigsaw of a puzzle this drowning was turning out to be. She took out paper and pen and wrote down whom she thought might possibly help her find answers to her questions. Dirk Nolten's son, Reinier, would, of course, be the logical first choice for finding out more about him. She thought that he would also be willing to keep her abreast of his father's condition because of their already established teacher-student bond. Yet, in her mind, getting him involved like this would be abusing their relationship. It might not be unethical, but it was certainly unkind. And she didn't want to be unkind to any of her students, not if she could help it. No, it was better to keep her distance and not bother the young man after his father's arrest. 'Definitely not him,' she mumbled, crossing out his name.

'Whatcha doing, Mama?' Femke was dragging around a stuffed reindeer sent by Kieran's mother in Ireland with the message: 'Can't wait to see our little muppet!'

'Come here,' she said to her daughter and gave her a kiss on the cheek. 'You're just too darn cute, and that reindeer of yours looks more like a big floppy moose. How nice of Nana Bridget to send it to you.'

She held it up to her mother for a closer look. 'I know, but whatcha doing?'

'I'm making a list of witnesses and suspects,' she said with a wink.

'Am I on it?'

'No, liefje. I don't suspect you of anything.'

'Is that a list for Santa?'

'Hmm, what a good idea. Do you think Santa could help me? I'm flummoxed.' The little girl ran off and returned shortly, handing her a red and blue box of chewable peppermint tablets. 'What's this?' said Felly.

'Papa says they're good for stomachs.'

'Oh,' she said, laughing. 'Flummox means to be confused. But thank you. Papa's right. They are good for tummy aches.'

'Mama, I'm bored. Can we go for a bike ride?'

Felly sighed over her paltry list of names that had included the one she had just crossed out. Pascal was on it too, but she thought he had already left to go skiing in the Alps. And then there was Sebastian De Vos. Except for him wanting her to check on the house right after the drowning, which she thought odd, there was nothing that she could see that would link him to anything out of the ordinary. And how about Trudi? The woman had already told her just about everything she had wanted to know, though Felly still felt that she was holding something back. Perhaps she could question her more about those secondary school years with Evi. Maybe even get her to dig out some old photographs of their class days. But would Trudi even be home? Most everyone had already left for the holidays, but it wouldn't hurt to check and see. She could give her a call and then maybe cycle over with Femke. 'You know what, poppie? I think a bike ride might be just what we need. But we'll have to bundle up. It's getting nippy outside.'

Femke immediately began putting on boots and pulling her coat off the wall rack as her mother Googled Trudi's address. Like many other university colleagues, the woman didn't live far from campus. Certainly not too far a distance for her and her daughter to reach on their bicycles. Instead of phoning, she thought it might be better to send a text, which would seem less intrusive for a last-minute query about a quick visit. Trudi surprisingly texted back as soon as she had received the message, replying that she didn't mind at all and would love to meet her little girl. 'What luck,' said Felly aloud to no one. She grabbed a tin box of sugar cookies from the pantry and stuck a bow on top before shoving it in a decorative plastic bag. Then they were off.

Opposite Trudi's rowhouse was the Kooipark, its landscaped grounds forming a grassy field, huge pond and wooden play area. When Femke saw it, she begged her mother if she could go off and play. 'Let's first visit my colleague, who's expecting us. We want to give her these cookies, don't we? Afterwards, I'll take you over to the swing and slide.'

She eyed the play area with longing, trying her best not to pout but doing so anyway. 'Look, Mama, a wooden bridge you can walk across.'

'Yes, it's all very creative.'

'Promise you'll take me.'

Felly crossed her heart. 'I promise.' Then she knocked on the door. When Trudi answered, Femke stepped up and presented her with the tin tied up with a bow in plastic bag.

The elder woman opened her door wider, smiling. 'What's this? For me?'

Femke beamed then took on a more serious tone. 'I'm Femke. Happy Christmas.'

'What a delightful child. I see the family resemblance. Thank you, Femke.'

'Honestly, everyone thinks she's the image of her father,' Felly said.

'Then he must be a handsome man.'

'We think he is.' She smiled lovingly at her daughter, who was now giggling. 'But, shhh, we never tell him that, do we, poppie.'

The little girl shook a headful of curls under her pink knitted cap. ''Cause he'll get seated.'

'He'll get what?'

'She means conceited, but she didn't hear that from me.'

'I'm sure that she did,' said the other woman, laughing. 'Well, come in and warm up. The sun might be shining, but the outside air is crisp. I was out earlier, myself, and I felt it go right through my bones.'

'Nippy,' said Femke, remember her mother's words.

Trudi held her smile. 'I've got a pot of tea brewing, but I can make coffee as well.'

'Tea's good,' said Felly. She rubbed her cold hands and blew on them. 'And thanks for letting us drop by. I hope we didn't disrupt any plans.'

'None at all, and I'm glad for the company. Baas is still finishing up at school.'

'Still?'

'Yes, please sit. So, is it tea then?' Felly nodded, yes. 'Cream and sugar?'

'One lump, please. No milk.'

'What would you like, Femke? I have juice, hot chocolate?'

She smiled up at the tall lady. 'Yummy, hot chocolate.'

They entered the living room with blue floral carpets half covering double parquet panelled flooring. Felly stopped to admire the surroundings then sat with her daughter on a grey cushioned sofa. 'You live with Dr De Vos?'

'For several years now.' She brought out a tea set and protective child's cup half-full of warmed up chocolate milk. 'I thought this was common knowledge.'

'You'll have to forgive my ignorance, not being from your department.'

'Oh, right. I keep forgetting you're one of the linguists. I hope you don't mind the Sippy cup, young miss. My granddaughters use them all the time.'

'I don't mind.'

'And what else do you say?' her mother reminded.

'Thank you,' she said, taking the cup and drinking from it.

Felly looked around, at the well-polished furnishings and tasteful paintings on the walls. 'You have a beautifully decorated home. Mine is more like a hodgepodge.'

'It makes a difference when you don't have kids. Ours are grown up, and the grandchildren seldom visit. They live in Friesland now.'

'Oh? Do you speak Fries with them?'

'No, I never learnt it. It was Nienke's father who was Fries, and she picked up bits and pieces growing up. She loves it there, which is probably why she ended up marrying a Frisian too.'

'Did you all live in Friesland back then?'

She poured tea, handing Felly a delicate cup with a decorative floral design. 'Gerrit and I lived here in Leiden. He died fourteen years ago.'

'My condolences.'

'We had a good life together. So, I have no regrets. And how about you? Have you always lived here?'

'Born and bred.'

'I'm surprised. I detect a bit of an anglified accent. With your daughter too.'

Felly smiled at that. 'Must be my Irish husband's influence. Femke also speaks Gaelic...as well as English.'

Trudi's hazel eyes settled on the little girl, whose upper lip now had a chocolate moustache. 'Aren't you the clever one, just like your mother.'

Femke only smiled. 'Mama says I can play on your playground slide too.'

The other woman laughed. 'Children, such delights.'

Felly laughed with her. 'So, do you still have family left in Den Bosch?'

She shook her head as she drank from her cup. 'Sadly, no. It's just me and Nienke now. And, of course, her husband, Jan, and the three grandchildren, Floris, Marlous and Aukie, who I'll bet is Femke's age.' She sized up the little girl. 'I'm guessing you're five years old. Am I right?'

Femke held up a hand and spread out all five fingers. 'But I'm gonna be six.'

'Time flies, yes?'

'It certainly does.'

'Evi was my only Den Bosch connection from those days. There are other classmates still alive, of course, but only acquaintances whom I wouldn't recognise even if I'd bump into them buying groceries.'

'It's so sad about Evi. I hardly knew her, myself. Were you two in any clubs together at school?'

Trudi let the sharp edges of her helmet hairdo fall past her ears as she looked briefly to the floor before looking up again. 'We were both so artistic back then, always good with our hands. We found each other doing set design for a school play before forming a drama club.'

'Did you both perform then?'

'No, nothing like that, just behind the scenes stuff. We became quite good at it, though, and had a lot of fun doing it.'

'Nice. My brother and I were in a few plays. We only had bit parts. But my parents were supportive, always spotting us onstage and taking pictures.'

'I think I have a few photos of us somewhere too.' She rose and went into the back room, returning with a shoebox which she set down on a small round table with wrought iron legs. 'Oh, here we were, constructing the set for 'Vaderje Langbeen', 'Daddy Longlegs'. And this was the one,' she showed Felly, 'where we had designed, yes, I believe this was a Christmas play.' She blinked as if in memory, then pointed to what looked like a wooden animal trough. 'But we got Evi's boyfriend, Dirk, to build that trough for the manger scene.'

'Dirk? As in Dirk Nolten?'

She nodded her head, smiling. 'Do you know him?'

'Uh, we've met.'

She turned back to the box and rummaged more till finding and pulling out another picture. 'There he is next to Evi. They were quite an item all throughout gymnasium.

Ach, we were so young and good looking then. So much life was ahead of us then.'

Felly recognised the face she was pointing to as Reinier's and took a deep breath. 'Talk about a child looking like a parent. He looks identical to his son.'

'Oh, I forgot that Reinier Nolten was taking your sociolinguistics course. Pascal said how much he'd enjoyed working with you all. What a pity the boy's father is having him transferred to Erasmus.'

'Trudi, you told me earlier that Evi had got pregnant as a teen and had to give the baby up for adoption. Dirk Nolten's baby?'

Trudi flushed, eyeing the picture again and blinking more. 'How thick am I, Felly? It's been staring me in the face all this time.'

'Meaning Dirk being the father of Evi's son?'

'Oh my, yes.'

'Is it possible for me to borrow this photo? I'll take very good care of it, I promise.'

'What do you want to do with it?'

'I just want to show it to someone.'

Trudi thought for a moment before rising from her chair. She held onto the back rest and sighed, long and hard. 'You'll have to excuse me, I ....' She paused, then said, 'Yes, take the photo, please.' Then she rushed mother and daughter to the door as they madly threw on scarves and coats.

'Mama?' said Femke, now outside still buttoning her coat.

'Oh my gosh, poppie. I'm sorry for that.'

They then grabbed their bicycles and wheeled them over to the park, Femke still looking at her mother. 'That lady is funny.'

'That's a good way to describe it.'

'Can I play on the slide now?'

'Go ahead. I'm right behind you.' Felly watched her daughter scamper to the wooden structure and climb onto its built-in slide. She slid down, laughing gleefully. Felly smiled back, as if in envy as she studied the photo in hand before pocketing it. 'What a world, what a world,' she muttered aloud. And it wasn't long till the chill in the air broke into snowflakes that softly danced through the air, picking up rhythm. 'Femke!' she called to her daughter still playing. 'We've got to go now.'

Kieran was home at their return. He greeted them with a smile as they shook snow off their coats before hanging them up to dry. 'And what have my two favourite girls been up to this afternoon? There's colour in yer cheeks.'

'I went on a big slide, Papa! But we gotsta go when the snow came.'

'A big slide?' He smiled broadly. 'That's just grand.' He helped her out of her boots and watched her skip off to see the cats. Then over to Felly, kissing her frozen lips. 'How can life get any better?'

She kissed him back, brushing a tear from her eye. 'Yer shaking, darlin'? He placed both arms around her and held her close. 'Winter's definitely here. I feel it too.'

'And I've got something to show you. But I don't know who else should see it. I have to think about this very carefully. Shall we sit down with a cup of tea, and I'll show it to you?'

'Already made and in the carafe.' He reached for the flannel fleece blanket draped over the couch and wrapped it around her. 'Warm yerself up and I'll pour us both a cupper.' He returned shortly with two hot mugs and set them down on the coffee table. 'Okay then, what have ye got to show me?'

She took the photo out of her bag, staring at the well-worn Polaroid before handing it to him.

'So, what am I looking at?' He scratched his dark blond hair. 'Kids at a Christmas party?'

'You remember meeting my student Reinier?'

'Oh right. He's in a play here with some friends. Sunday school days?'

'That's his dad, Kieran. Dirk Nolten.'

'Doppelgangers, I'd say.' He turned the photo round between thumb and forefinger, inspecting its yellowed edges. 'Where did it come from?'

'Femke and I paid a visit to Trudi Langmeijer before the slide adventure in the park. Trudi is De Vos's secretary. I just found out they live together, but no matter. That's not important.'

He snuggled up close, taking some of the offered blanket. 'And this is from her?'

'Remember me telling you that she and Evi were secondary school classmates? It turns out that Evi was also dating Dirk at the time.'

'Our man, Dirk?'

'The very one. Evidently, he and Evi were quite the pair, what the English call high school sweethearts.'

He furrowed his brows, thinking.

'Don't you see the connection, Kieran?'

'No, but yer going to clue me in, right?'

She pressed her hands to her cheeks. 'I think Pascal is Dirk's son.'

'Oh, I see.' Long pause. 'May I borrow this?'

'Of course. Trudi wants it back, though. At least, I think she does.'

150

He turned to her and kissed her lips. 'The world may be wicked, darlin', but we still have each other. Just remember that. And Femke. And them devil cats.'

'C'mon, Kier,' she said grinning. 'I saw you cuddling Pip on your lap last night.'

'Jayzus, girl, don't be tellin' that to everyone.'

'Your secret's safe with me, you old soft-hearted fool.'

'I married ye, didn't I?' he teased.

'And I married you, fool that I am too.'

'Ye did, indeed. So, who's the bigger fool?'

They both looked up at the same time when hearing a visibly upset Femke in the hall. She came in crying with face cream and powder running down her face. 'I was just 'tending to be a snowman and it got stuck on me.'

Felly rolled her eyes. 'Oh poppie.' She rose from the couch, taking her by the hand. 'I'm going to show you how to clean up, but I'm letting you do it all by yourself this time. Is that a deal?'

Femke nodded, still in tears. Kieran shot his wife a sidewise glance, laughing. 'Just another afternoon in fools' paradise.'

Dirk Nolten was about to be released on his own recognizance when Kieran made his call to the station, leaving house shortly after and taking Trudi's photograph with him. Kieran hoped to catch the man before he left for Den Bosch. And, like water from the eaves, as the Dutch say, Felly wished more than ever that she could be an eavesdropper and listen in on their conversation. Fate was cruel, however; her fate of being married to a counsellor who was representing the one she so desperately wanted to question. Yet, she respected client-lawyer confidentiality. And, tempted though she was, Felly would never look into any of her husband's files on Dirk Nolten. Nor would she take a peek at his emails. No correspondence would be looked at that wasn't mutual. She would have to be patient, which was admittedly not her strong suit. Meanwhile, a mother-daughter outing was planned with Christmas shopping on the square.

Oma Ankie greeted her daughter and granddaughter at a kiosk where Felly and Kieran had been meeting for coffee over the years when on short breaks from school and work. Today the ladies skipped the coffee and walked together between the stalls, eyeing dried fruits and nuts, sampling cheeses and poking through holiday floral displays from outlying flower farms. Felly stopped to buy Femke a warm waffle and was giving it to her when she caught sight of her colleague strolling by. 'Well, hello, there,' she called out. 'I thought you were off skiing.'

Pascal smiled her way. 'Hoi, you two. And I thought you'd be gone to Ireland by now.'

'We're spending Christmas Eve with the folks first. I don't think you've met my mother, Anneke.'

He came closer and eyed the sporty looking blonde woman standing next to her. 'The apple doesn't fall far from the tree in your family.'

'And who is this handsome fellow?' Her mother played along in light flirtation.

'My colleague, Pascal.'

'I've picked up a few things that'll pass for a casual dinner,' he told them. 'Well, lunch, maybe. A kind of dinner-lunch.'

'It's called tea or supper in English,' said Ankie.

'Be that as it may, wine is the intended main course. And I've just purchased these munchables to go with it.' He held up a see-through bag of hummus spreads, olives and exotic looking crackers from the Ilias Delicatessen, a kiosk they'd just passed.

'It all looks tasty to me, said Felly's mother. 'Have you purchased your intended wine yet? If not, I'd recommend an earthy red, like Pinot Noir.'

'Already on it.' He grinned and held up the sack in his other hand.

'So, when are you leaving town? I'd like to chat with you about something before you go. We'll be at the folks on Tuesday and are flying to Cork Christmas morning. Anytime before that we should be home, though.'

'Is it urgent?' he said.

She shrugged. 'It could be.'

Felly's mother screwed up her face. 'Could you be any more evasive, schat?'

'Well, I was planning to eat this alone. I could bring it over if you're not doing anything this afternoon. Does Kieran like hummus?'

Both ladies looked at each other and laughed. 'Kieran likes anything, but, yes. We're free. Say five-ish?'

'Super. I'll be there. Bye, Femke,' he said to the little girl who had locked her eyes on him. Then he walked off and melted into the crowded market square.

'My word, now that's a looker,' said Anneke. 'You do lead an interesting life.'

'Oh, Ma, stop.'

Kieran was home when Felly and Femke returned from their shopping day which ended with a pleasant coffee at a terrace café on the square. Femke had talked her grandmother into ordering hot chocolate with whipped cream and holiday sprinkles. After that, and the waffle she ate while walking around with her mother, she was full and wanted nothing more when she got home than to relax and play on her iPad. Felly left her all snug in her room with cats underfoot, then went in search of Kieran. She found him in his small study, paperwork all round.

'I bumped into Pascal today. Or, we, I should say. My mother joined us for some Christmas shopping.'

Kieran looked up tired-eyed and seemingly distracted. 'Pascal, from work?'

'Mmhm, and he's bringing over some Turkish spreads he bought, which I hope will be accompanied with that nice bottle of red wine he purchased too.'

Kieran sighed. 'This is not the best time. I had a somewhat taxing morning that I'm trying to get all sorted. I was hoping for a quiet rest of the day with just family.'

'Does your present mood have anything to do with Dirk Nolten and that picture I leant you?'

'Ye know I can't say.'

She clicked her tongue to the roof of her mouth. 'You didn't leave the photo with him, did you?'

'Of course not. Are ye planning to show it to Pascal?'

She nodded her head, yes.

'Felly, I don't think that's such a good idea?'

'He has a right to know, Kier.'

'But is it yer right to tell him?'

She eyed her phone, sighing. 'I see. Or at least I think I understand what you're not telling me, what you can't discuss.'

He only shrugged and looked away.

'You think I should call it off then?'

'That might be wise.'

She sighed, staring at her phone. 'I'm finding all this conflicting...conflicting with the truth even...maybe...even.'

'All I can say is that what I thought would be a simple B&E is turning into a damn good case.'

'Oh, my God. I knew it.'

'I'm sorry it has to be this way, darlin', but I truly can't discuss anything more with ye right now.'

'That's fine then.' There was no other word for it, just 'sad', a sad state of affairs.

'Papa,' cried Femke from her bedroom. 'Can I have some stomach mints?'

'Are you flummoxed too, poppie?'

'Yes, my tummy hurts.'

Felly sighed. 'That makes two of us with a flummoxed stomach.'

12

Dirk Nolten was out on bail and knew that he had a lot of explaining to do to his family but hadn't gone home just yet. He had checked into a hotel to give himself a breather and gather his wits. At this point, he really didn't know what to do or how to go about it. After the awkwardly painful conversation with his solicitor, McNeela, in the station holding cell, a social worker had also come round before he was released. She had offered her services with family counselling, which only made him flush with anger. Did everyone know his business now? He knew he should not have gone to Evi's house in search of her kept letters, or any other damning evidence he might find. And now Kieran's Polaroid photograph, which caused him to gasp with disbelief. Where had the man got hold of it? He wouldn't tell him but only wanted to discuss it, which opened a floodgate of measured confession that left him feeling drained and his soul empty. He now felt betrayed by life and his present circumstances and refused to discuss anything more with anyone.

Dirk balled up his fist and beat on his thigh. Stupid, stupid, stupid. How could he not have recognised his own flesh and blood back then? How had he let this happen? Admittedly, Evi's offspring looked more like her than him, but the man who he recognised in the restaurant had taken his breath away just the same. He wished to rise above it all and think pleasant thoughts. Yet, he felt damned. What he had unwittingly done was to him unspeakable, unthinkable to even mention. And these days he was another person, a church-going man and integral part of his community. Life was the devil...now seemingly so meaningless after this buried past had cruelly crept up on him and ruined it. He lowered his head and covered his eyes with one hand. No, this couldn't have happened, not to him, not to Dirk Nolten, family man. It had happened to another, a younger person and other life. He didn't want to be reminded of it, nor have it dragged out in public. His family now knew about the breaking and entering. And they would ask questions. What was he going to tell them? He had no answers, and no backup plan to cover his bases. He simply couldn't think.

He opened the hotel room mini bar and peered in, seeing it stocked full of beverages, Red Bull energy drink, orange juice, bottled water and assorted beers. He went for the harder stuff on the side door, opening a small chilled bottle of Smirnoff, which only gave him a slight buzz. He took a well-needed shower then caught the lift down to the hotel bar where he ordered Absolut, neat. He continued to run a tab and sat there thinking, musing over his damned accursed life. His anger mounting instead of subsiding. Damn that Pascal, damn him to hell.

After a good hour at the bar, Dirk decided to go back to his room and sleep off the drink. This was his intention, and a very good one, he thought. Sound and sane, as he had taught himself to be. 'What you need to be,' he said aloud to the empty room, 'to get along in this mad, mad, dog-eat-dog world.'

He looked in the fridge again. And, against his better judgement, opened a whiskey sampler, killing the bottle. The room now seemed more like a prison to him, a four-walled (albeit cleaner) cell than the one he had been in until that morning. 'Fuhk 'de zooi.' I'm outta here!'

He grabbed his jacket and slipped in his phone, his wallet and keys. Then he left in search of Pascal, intending only talk to him, his, oh my God, son! Perhaps Pascal had given the photograph to Kieran McNeela. If so, then he and the lawyer had some explaining to do.

It wasn't easy to track down someone he hardly knew, and one who by an odd twist of fate had also been his son's university professor. A quick call to Reinier would give him the information he sought, a phone number to contact. But, no, he wouldn't dream of getting Reinier involved. Instead, he took the lift back to the lobby and asked to use a public computer where he could search online for an address. Easily finding what he was looking for, he wrote everything down that directed him to an apartment complex in Amsterdam Sloterdijk, a 30-minute drive north. Dirk used the Uber app on his phone to hail a driver, then instructed her to take him there and wait.

He still felt the alcohol in his system, but not as strong now as he knocked on the apartment door, fingers trembling. An attractive Moluccan man around the same age as Pascal answered. 'I'm looking for Pascal,' said Dirk, slurring his words.

'He hasn't lived here in ages. Why don't you ask his parents?' And he slammed the door in Dirk's face.

'A fuhking waste of a dead-end,' Dirk muttered aloud. 'Fuhk, fuhk, fuhk!' He had the driver bring him back to his hotel, where, with the use of an online telephone guide, he began another search. The guide displayed a half dozen van Houten surnames, ignoring those with female sounding given names and concentrating on the males and those with simple initials. He called everyone until a friendly elder man's voice answered, acknowledging Pascal as his son. Dirk answered in like manner, passing himself off as an acquaintance who had planned to meet him that evening but had forgotten the address. 'But it's at the Café Barrera,' the voice on the end said somewhat baffled. 'Everyone knows it, son. Just look it up.' Dirk apologised what he thought a pathetic sounding thanks before hanging up and Ubering another ride.

As he sat in the back of the silver Hyundai, Dirk practiced the dialogue he imagined he would be having when face-to-face with Pascal. His initial intentions were only to have a chat, maybe even apologise for the long-ago fling while never dreaming that this would be with his then still teenaged son. Even the thought of it now sickened him beyond belief. He clenched the armrest and breathed deeply, in and out, in and out. When he left the Uber and approached the café's ebony double doors, it looked to Dirk as if the place was catering to a full house. Interior lighting was strung festively across the ceiling, which stung his bloodshot eyes. And the throbbing sounds of music coupled with thrumming human chatter caused him to press his hands to his ears and listen to the pounding within. 'How can I track down anyone in this chaos?'

This was precisely when Dirk spotted his son. Reinier had been milling around campus, unable to tear himself away from his friends. He had not even packed his bags for home, but procrastinated until he could no longer put off the day, the moment, when he would have to leave it all behind. Seeing Reinier now, appearing so blissfully unaware and happy, Dirk felt a stabbing pang of guilt. How could he have done this to his own son, tearing him away from all this? He felt awful, more than the scum between the ridges of the soles of his shoes. Reinier was, of course, unaware of anything that had been happening to his father these past few days. His university life was another world, another existence than his elder father's present hell. Yet, Dirk did a doubletake when he caught sight of who his son was sharing a beer with. And if all the festive lights could burn and pop they would be doing so now.

Dirk rushed over to the unsuspecting duo, Pascal having no idea what he was getting into as he smiled in recognition at the approach of his now ex-student's father. The blind-sightedness was Kieran's doing, as he had convinced Felly not to further entangle herself in what he could only confide was an extremely sensitive issue. Thus, Pascal had no clue when he mistakenly thought Reinier's father was seeking them out to clarify the decision for the switch in universities. He was sorry to see the lad go, though it made sense to send Reinier to Erasmus, which in Pascal's mind was another fine university for those studying finance.

Dirk's anger was thundering when he reached the two sons, neither recognising the other as being so. And before Pascal could even say a word, Dirk delivered a blow with such force that it knocked him to the ground. Reinier stared in disbelief before letting out a scream. 'Bloody hell, Dad! What the fuck! Get off him!'

Dirk kept punching as he spewed his hatred, hatred at the world, hatred at life. He cursed all this hateful

161

nonsense at him, his other son. Reinier was now crying while trying to pull his father off his teacher, as others looked on with dropping jaws. Neither could Pascal make head nor tail of it all before passing out.

At this point, the police had been called in, as well as an ambulance. And the stupefied Reinier saw his father, Dirk, hauled off to the station as his professor, Pascal, was taken to hospital.

13

Pascal suffered a mild concussion, a few broken ribs and multiple bruises. He was confused when he woke up, drugged, and in pain as he tried to sit up in bed. He lay back down on the starched pillow he had been lying on, his fingers slowly checking out his face. With thin laughter, he said, 'At least I'm not disfigured.'

A bronze-skinned man about his age was sitting by the side of his bed. 'You're all right, man,' he said. 'I mean, you will be once your ribs heal. And you'll have some discolouration, but not on your face.'

'Xander?' his voice spoke out in surprise. 'What are you doing here? I'm okay, aren't I? I still have all my functioning parts?'

'I wouldn't know about that. You'll have to ask the last guy you slept with,' the other chuckled softly. 'But I don't think you'll be skiing anytime soon.'

'You heard about my vacation plans? What? Through my parents?'

'Yes, and I'm sorry.' He reached over and gently clasped his free arm, the one that wasn't hooked to an IV. 'I feel half responsible for what happened to you.'

Pascal looked baffled. 'What? Why is that?'

'I shouldn't have said one word to that mad man, not one word.'

'Who are you talking about?' Pascal looked nervously about the room, relaxing again when he didn't see anyone other than the two of them there, him and his old partner, Xander Anakotta. 'I'm doing my best to remember, but I'm only drawing blanks. Can you fill me in?'

'Some old guy came to the apartment looking for you, old but fit like in that construction workout kind of way. He was also scary drunk. I shut the door in his face, shouting for him to go ask your parents. I guess he did.'

'You're still mad at me for leaving, aren't you?'

'Yeah, as a matter of fact, I am. So, why did you? You were never all that clear.'

'I don't know. It was getting intense between us, and I just ran.'

'You ran home, you mean?'

'I ran home, yes...like a coward.'

'You sure are. But I'd like to save that talk for later.' He ran the back of his hand across Pascal's face, reached down and kissed him. 'I miss you, man, but you suck at relationships.'

They both laughed, Pascal wincing and groaning. 'I owe you a huge apology. You could do better than me, anyway.'

'Let me be the judge of that,' said Xander. 'Your parents were here earlier, by the way. And some gorgeous woman dropped in who claimed she worked with you.'

Pascal nodded as best he could. Even if his face weren't damaged, he was still sore all over. 'Must have been my colleague, Felly.'

'She was beside herself, telling me she also felt responsible.'

'Why is everyone feeling guilty about what happened to me? Feel free to clue me in.'

Xander shrugged. 'All I know is that this fit guy laid into you when he saw you talking to his son. Were you hitting on one of your students? Not too smart, Paz.'

Bits and pieces began flooding back in Pascal's memory. 'No, I wasn't hitting on Reinier. He's definitely straight, and his girlfriend is too.'

'Okay, my bad. Something pissed off the old man.'

'I remember seeing him and thinking he was coming over to talk with me about Reinier leaving for another college.'

'Huh.' He shook his head, puzzling. 'Someone called the police, and they hauled the guy off before he murdered you. That's all I know. The pretty lady said she'd be back later. Maybe she can tell you more.'

'Thanks, man,' Pascal wiped his eyes. 'Jeezus, look at me all teary-eyed. What the hell is wrong with me?'

'Other than being beaten to a pulp?' said Xander, grinning sidewise. 'A lot.' And he reached down and kissed him again. 'I've got to go to work. Would you mind if I come by later? I'd like to have that talk.'

'Yes, I'd like that too.' He watched his old partner leave the room, thinking how attractive he still was. 'What an oaf I was to run from you, Xander,' he muttered aloud to the hospital walls. 'A stupid oaf.'

Felly returned to the hospital after having had a long discussion with Kieran over how she thought them both culpable to a certain extent. 'This could've been avoided if we'd only had Pascal over the other night like I'd planned,' she told him.

He strongly disagreed, saying, 'The fault wasn't ours, darlin'. It's been Dirk's and the choices he's been making all along. No one solves anything with their fists, and he's got himself in a right mess now.' He also disagreed about showing Pascal the Polaroid. 'I don't think it's our place to intrude,' he said, 'in a conversation that should be between yer man and his father.'

She caught the slip. 'So, you admit it!'

He only sighed. 'Don't quote me, girl.'

'I agree that it would have been nice if Dirk Nolten had had the guts to open up to Pascal. It would have been the decent thing for him to do, but I don't see him doing it anytime soon. Do you?'

Kieran shrugged. 'Perhaps it's just the mettle of the man. It takes courage to be honest.'

'Yes, it does. Honesty can be a bitch sometimes.'

He smiled. 'To put it in layman's terms, yes. And something to think about when ye go flashing that photo around. Not everyone can take it.'

'I know,' she said. 'But Pascal has the right to know. Now more than ever. And what happens next will no doubt be influenced by him wanting to press charges, or not, for the violent attack.'

'Yer right in that. So's....'

'So's?' She smiled.

He kissed her, eyeing her lovingly. 'Good luck, darlin''

En-route to the hospital, Felly thought it also wise to keep Trudi in the loop. She knew her call would upset the woman, who was most likely regretting the lending of the photo. Yet, Felly believed that it was in the harbouring of secrets that had turned everything into such a domino effect of lies, deceits and coverups, resulting in the current state they were all in. What she wasn't sure of was how much more she should be personally involved. Kieran had placed some serious doubts in her mind, this fierce loyalty of his being something tribal, something Celtic. It was also a feature that had attracted her to him, initially, knowing deep down that he would be always looking out for her welfare, hers and Femke's.

She entered the hospital and stopped first by the florist to pick out a holiday bouquet, choosing one with frosted greenery, red roses, pine cones and berries. 'This will cheer up, Pascal,' she said as she swiped her pin card over a countertop machine. He wasn't alone when she came into the room, not as she hoped he would be. Reinier and Minke were also visiting, having given him a beautiful bouquet of their own, now displayed in a vase on the rolling tray table next to the bed. She quickly tucked back in the photo she had taken out of her purse, deciding to show it to him later. Then she presented the flowers to him while greeting Reinier and Minke. 'Hello, you two. All set for the holidays?'

'Yes,' they said. 'We had to stop by and pay our favourite professor a visit first. Then we're off to Den Bosch. No hard feelings, Professor McNeela.'

'None taken,' she smiled back. 'He's my favourite professor too.'

'I was planning on skiing, myself,' said Pascal, which caused polite laughter.

This was when Reinier took Felly aside, saying, 'I'd like to speak with you about something.' He looked at his girlfriend who was all decked in red for the holidays, and at Pascal, still wearing tight bandages around his chest. 'Do you mind if we go grab some coffee?'

'Not if you're planning on bringing us back some,' Minke said with a wink.

Pascal piped in. 'Make mine cappuccino.'

'Will do. Oh, and you can leave your stuff here, Professor,' he told her. 'I'm picking up the tab.'

'Thank you. That's sweet of you.'

She took off her jacket and threw it and her purse atop the empty bed beside Pascal's, then walked with Reinier down the hall to the cafeteria. 'I just wanted to cheer up the poor guy, but you're my favourite professor too.'

'I wasn't offended,' she said with a smile. 'So, tell me, you were right there too, witnessing everything. That must have been awful for you.'

He nodded his head. 'I hadn't seen my father for days, not after his insisting that I go to Erasmus, which I still haven't transferred to, by the way. I'm putting my foot down on this one. I'm staying at Leiden U.'

'That's wonderful news. But is that all you wanted to talk to me about?'

'No, that was just the half of it,' he said. 'After what happened last night, Dad losing his mind and going ballistic, I followed him to the police station. First no one would even let me see him. So, I stayed and waited till they did.'

'Oh my gosh. You should have called. I would have come and waited with you.'

'Thanks, but I was okay. I just needed to speak to my father and ask him what was going on. I mean, what the hell?'

'And did they finally let you see him?'

They were at the cafeteria now. So, they stopped to order two coffees and cappuccinos to go. Then they sat together at a plastic table, drinking gingerly from their very hot cups. 'I finally got it all out of him, Professor.'

'Please, you can call me Felly now.'

'Okay, Felly. I finally got Dad to tell me that Pascal is my brother.'

She let out her breath. 'Well, I'm glad to hear that.'

He eyed her with uncertainty. 'Did you already know this?'

She nodded her head. 'I knew but couldn't say. My husband is your father's lawyer, you know.'

'He is?' Now Reinier was completely baffled. 'When did all this happen? I must have been sleeping.'

'It's been quite the chain of events, I assure you. Coupled with that is my inability to disclose much of anything without the possibility of getting in hot water over it. So, I have to be so careful too, but I'm glad your father told you. That must have been hard for him to do.'

'Yeah, I could tell by the look on his face that he was carrying a lot of shame over it too, even though it happened so long ago. I mean, Pascal is ancient. He's got to be in his late twenties.'

She laughed. 'Something like that.'

'I asked Dad why he went off on him like he did. I mean, that's not what you do to your long-lost son.' Reinier shook his head, drinking from his cup.

'No, it's not.'

'I could tell Dad was drunk. But the way he acted? That was just insane.'

'He was under a lot of pressure. Maybe he just cracked.'

'Nothing justifies the way he acted. It was humiliating being his son just then, and I told him so too.'

'Oh? How did he take that?'

He gave her a sidewise smile. 'As you can imagine. He did say, and I think I believe him, that he didn't even know about Pascal being his son. He said he didn't know until recently. Otherwise, he said things would have been different.'

'I see. And did he say anything else?'

'Only that he was sorry. And then he started sobbing. I knew it was the alcohol because I've never seen him like that before, never.'

'I'm sorry you had to see your father like that too,' she said. 'So, how are you now? How are you processing all this?'

'Admittedly, it's going to take awhile. I've got Minke's support too, which I suppose I have you and your project to thank for getting us together.'

Felly beamed. 'You're welcome. Shall we head back now before the cappuccinos get cold?'

Reinier rose from his cafeteria stool. 'Thanks for hearing me out. It helps talking to someone else about all this.'

'Anytime, Reinier. I mean that.'

When they re-entered the room, Minke and Pascal were laughing together. 'I'm glad you're back,' Pascal complained. 'Your girlfriend's killing me with her jokes.'

'Leave the poor man alone,' laughed Reinier. 'Here, brother.' He handed Pascal one of the cappuccinos and the other to Minke. 'Well, I guess we'd better be going. Mom's expecting us for dinner, and we need to catch a train.'

'Have a good holiday,' Felly told them both, adding a brief wave as they headed out the door.

170

'So, I have a brother,' said Pascal all smiles. 'Can you imagine that?'

'And don't forget Reinier's little sister, Rinske.'

'Oh, right.' He beamed. 'A half-sister too. This is going to be hard on Dirk's wife, though. I know it is for me. I'm still processing everything, myself.'

'That's just what Reinier told me.'

'And did the two of you end up having a good conversation?'

'Not only that but his decision to study at Leiden is a definite one. So, we'll see him next term.'

'I'm sure that didn't go down well with his hot-tempered father.'

'It's good for Reinier to take a stand. It builds character.'

'Perhaps he takes more after his mother then?'

They both snickered. Then Felly said, 'Pascal, I need to show you something that I should have shown you before. Before Dirk sought you out and slapped you around, to put it mildly.'

'If you mean the photograph, I already saw it.'

'You did?' She glimpsed the other bed, seeing her purse right where she left it, resting atop her winter coat. 'Did Kieran show you?'

'Kieran? Your husband? Why would he be showing me? No, it must have slipped out of your bag when you threw it on the bed. Minke picked it up off the floor, and we were laughing together about it.'

'Oh? Why would you be laughing about it?'

'Wasn't that Reinier in some secondary school play? It looks just like him.'

'No, Pascal, not Reinier. That's Trudi Langmeijer's old Polaroid. It's of her with Evi and his father...your father, Dirk Nolten.'

'So, there it is on Polaroid. No denying it now that I'm the bastard son of Evi Anneveldt, the bastard son who once had a tryst with his own father. Do you ever wonder some days why you were even born?' Pascal was now blinking away tears and groaning. 'What a mess, what a mess. Does Reinier know all this too?'

'I don't think so. And he doesn't have to know, Pascal. What good would it do him?'

'Only more harm than good,' he agreed. 'I just hope Minke doesn't ask him about the picture.'

'He wouldn't have a clue what she was talking about, and I'm not going to show him. The Polaroid's back in my purse, right?'

'Right.'

'And I'm returning it to Trudi. I'm not justifying what either your birthmother or father did, but those were different times. And neither even knew exactly who you were until such a disclosure might have complicated things more by disclosing it.'

'I still would have liked to have known. I mean, God, Felly, I would have never had been with my own father at the Blue River Sauna. How the hell? How unthinkable.'

She shook her head sadly. 'That was an unfortunate encounter for you both.'

'Which now makes sense how he released all his pent-up anger by making me his human punching bag.'

'Stupid man,' she said under her breath.

An older couple appeared in the room just then and introduced themselves as Pascal's parents. This was her excuse to part company. She put on her coat and clutched her purse, saying, 'Happy holidays, everyone.'

'And to you too,' they all replied.

Felly left the room thinking of a Dutch idiom: *We zullen wel zien waar het schip strandt.* 'Yes,' she murmured. 'We'll see where this ship beaches.'

14

Winter weather in the Netherlands was typically rainy and wet with near-freezing temperatures, but the streets glistened in lamplight that shone like muted gold, reminding Felly of fireflies skating across glazed concrete ponds. The wrought iron lamps above beamed a crimson yellow along walkways of elms and London plane trees now bejewelled in white light that marked out routes with their twinkling. She loved winter holiday season when even the dustiest of alleyways took on a romantic glow that stretched across an otherwise sombre cityscape. Despite the need to bundle up in everything warm you could think of, Felly thought it her favourite time of year.

On this Christmas Eve, the McNeelas were readying for dinner with the parents, and would be joined soon by Felly's brother and sister-in-law. They were also leaving for Ireland the following morning, flying together to Cork. And there they would part ways. Kieran, Felly and Femke would be taxiing to Youghal to be with his family for Christmas Day brunch; and Filip and Moira would travel on by train to

Kerry, where they would stay through Boxing Day with Moira's cousins, Aidan and Sean.

Pascal had only been heard from once since his twenty-four hour stay in hospital, which had been a precautionary measure to ensure nothing more serious would come of his mild concussion. Other than feeling headachy, his time of danger had passed and he was released with broken ribs that would heal on their own. His call to Felly was mostly to thank her for being there for him. He also gave her an update on his visit to whom he was now calling 'the pathetic Dirk Nolten', confiding to her that the decision he made was more for his own peace of mind. He said he wanted the contact to be while the man was still safely behind bars, assuring him of a captive audience.

'And how did that go?' she asked.

'After hearing me out, and me mulling over his limp apologies, I decided not to press assault charges.'

'That shows a lot of character on your part, Pascal.'

'Not really.' She heard him sigh. 'When we got together ten years ago it was a fluke, the attraction carnal in that cheap one-night-stand kind of way. I don't think either of us will ever recover from our later shock of recognition, of what we had done together. I mean, father and son? How could we have known that then? And we didn't, Felly. Oh my God, I swear we didn't. It was one of those dreadfully ironic accidents of life, or so we both agreed.'

She breathed out, expressing her condolences. 'I'm so sad that this has happened to you.'

'To dwell on it any further would do more harm than good. It would only festering like a cancer in the brain.'

'I'm proud of you, Pascal. That couldn't have been easy.'

'No, it wasn't. I only know that I am truly letting go, letting go and moving on. And I hope for his own sake that the pathetic Dirk Nolten does too.'

'In case you're wondering, I gave the Polaroid back to Trudi. I think she burned it.'

'Good riddance.' There was a moment of silence. Then on a cheerier note, Pascal said that he and Xander decided to give it another go. 'We're moving back in together on a trial basis.'

'That's wonderful news. He seems like a decent guy.'

'Baby steps,' he said with a slight cough.

'He told me he's a medical coder. What is that, anyway?'

'A professional number puncher,' he laughed.

She laughed too. 'I'm sure it's more involved than that.'

'Oh, it is. I just give him a hard time, but what he basically does is assign codes to diagnoses and procedures.'

'Sounds very technical.'

'You certainly have to have the brains for it.'

'He'll be a real challenge for you then. Well, dear man, happy Christmas to you both.'

'And to you too. Until next year,' he said and then hung up.

Felly was glad the air had been cleared for her colleague and wondered if it would be the same for his long-lost father. Dirk was a man from another generation and not, in her mind, the best of communicators. She also wondered what type of family reunion would be awaiting him at home in Den Bosch.

'A frosty one, I'd imagine,' said Kieran, who'd been listening in as he packed his bag atop their king-sized bed.

'I know you can't divulge anything that your client tells you. But I still think Dick Nolten pushed Evi Anneveldt into that canal to keep her quiet.'

'I think ye should take to heart Pascal's advice. Let it go, darlin'. It's Christmas, and I'm so looking forward to yer mam's cooking.'

'I don't think you'll be disappointed. She's planned quite the spread.' Then she shot a glance across the hall. 'Femke, are you just about ready?' she called.

The little girl came out wearing a red buffalo checked dress with an inset of white lace between the front buttons. 'That's a lovely choice, poppie, but it's cotton and may not be warm enough.'

'I am warm, Mama.'

She sighed. 'Then put on your wool leggings and fur-lined boots.'

'We are Ubering there,' Kieran reminded.

'Oh, right. Well, come here and let me fix your hair.' She deftly tucked the fine golden strands into a French braid as she searched through her cosmetic drawer and found a red clip-on bow to match. 'There, what do you think?'

Kieran eyed them both appreciatively. 'Stop the lights. I've got the two most gorgeous girls I've ever seen.'

Femke just beamed. 'We're gonna get seated, Papa.'

He glimpsed his wife, puzzling.

'She means conceited,' Felly laughed. 'So, are we all packed then? I think our ride's here.'

Kieran helped Femke first with her coat, then put on his own jacket. 'We're all sorted.'

'Then let's go. We're not in Ireland yet, and we don't want to be running late.'

'Off again, off again, jiggety jig,' sang Kieran merrily.
'We're going to the van Vliets....'

'To eat a fresh pig!' chimed in Femke.

Felly grew up in a house full of Irish Settters. She
and her brother Filip were raised by professional breeders,
now retired. Yet, this initial love of the breed had come
about by accident: actually, a car accident. Baby Anneke
had been teething and was too fussy to bring with her
parents one Sunday morning. So, Oma Ria had offered to
babysit to allow the daughter and son-in-law to have some
alone time together. Yet, this very act of kindness was one
that she would regret for the rest of her life, because a
drunk driver had hit and killed them both as they cycled on
their way to church.

Anneke Kok grew up never knowing her parents,
only the loving elders who had taken her in and raised her
as their own. As they aged, they feared the girl might grow
up somewhat isolated from others closer in age. So, they
continued to do volunteer work at their church, involving her
as well when she grew older. The teenage Anneke was
sporty, well-adjusted and sociable. She was also keeping
an eye peeled on an attractive schoolmate in the church
badminton team. At one of the matches, Martinus's parents
brought with them an attractive dog with a mahogany-
coloured coat, and Anneke just had to inquire after the
breed. The boy shyly told her it was his mother, Connie's,
doing. She had been an RAF nurse for the British forces
when she met his father, a wounded soldier in the Dutch
Resistance. They married shortly after Liberation Day, and
Connie brought with her to the Netherlands the parents of
the Irish Setter that Anneke stood admiring. Martinus
mostly liked the breed for its freedom-loving nature. And,

like the woman he eventually married, they were highly sociable creatures.

During school holidays, Felly and her brother Filip would help their parents on the dog show circuit. Being twins often drew attention, and this benefited the show animals as well. After the runt of the last litter had died, the van Vliets dropped out of this competitive arena with only their ribbons and photos left to decorate the walls of the attractive lime-brick home inherited from Tinus's parents and situated in an older section of town west of the old castle wall.

This Christmas Eve, Felly and her young family entered the big foyer and hung up their coats as caramelised odours of seasoned vegetables in oil and baked blood of frying steak accosted their senses.

'Drinks, everyone?' said Felly's father. 'Our little schatje first, of course. What will you have, Femke? Strawberry juice?'

'Strouberry, yes, please.' She followed her grandfather into the kitchen, switching to Dutch and continuing to speak it with him.

Anneke approached them, apron strung around her white crocheted blouse and black leggings. 'I've got whiskey on the counter, Kieran. And red wine is in the fridge, dear,' she said to her daughter. 'Just help yourselves and go join Filip and Moira. They're in the living room already.'

Felly headed to the large, American-sized refrigerator while her mother handed Kieran a whiskey glass. 'You're looking well and rested,' she said to him. 'Job going okay?'

'Going good, going good,' he said. 'Got a sad case I'm working on at the moment, though. I'm so looking forward to this holiday.'

She drank from her glass as she watched him pour his. 'I imagine those sad cases can be draining.'

'They absolutely are.' Then he lifted his glass to her. 'Proost.'

'And sláinte,' she replied. 'Bridget's going to love seeing our little granddaughter. How long has it been? Four months now?'

'Since last summer. And children grow like weeds, don't they?'

'I still remember mine in diapers,' she laughed.

He laughed with her. 'I won't pass that one on, but it must have been something for ye, raising twins. A handful, I imagine.'

'You imagine right. I was lucky in that Martinus has always been a great help, then and now. And when the kids got out of hand, I resorted to my dog training techniques.'

He snorted. 'What? Like sit, stay, heel?'

'Sounds pretty bad, now that I think about it. So don't pass that one on, either.'

'I won't, but it explains a lot.' He was still laughing when he went to join the others. Moira's voice rose above the rest. She was at it again with a sequel about her aunt and the kitchen trespassing goats.

'And then she says to me.' She looked up, winking at Kieran as she saw him come in. 'She says, dem goats was back again, Moira. This time the little shites went for the communion wafers, and I had nothin' for the priest that day. So, what'd ye do? I asked her. And she says back to me, Ah, for fecks sake. I crunched up some Italian breadsticks and called 'em papal leftovers. Papal leftovers? Ah me, Aunt Mary's gone plain mad this time, just plain mad.'

Dinner was served formally at the dining table, which was elegantly set with crystal and red linen napkins. There were frosted pine branches decorating the middle of the table with pine cones all round. The steaks were served according to preference, rare, medium or well-done, along with baked potatoes. Felly wasn't much of a meat eater and ended up sharing hers with Femke, who, like her father, wanted to taste a little of everything.

Everyone was well-sated when the meal was over, coffee being served by a cheerfully burning hearth fire. In honour of the Irish Kieran and Moira, and the half-Irish Femke, a log of peat had been purchased and was now warming their toasty feet as they continued sharing in conversation while awaiting the *Nachtmis*, or Christmas Eve mass.

And when the hour came, they sat in the pews and listened to the organ music playing. What Felly loved best was that she and Kieran had been married in this church, which was also the day that she had found out she was pregnant. Far from being a virgin birth, hers was out of love flamed with passion. And like this evening's peat fire, she thought with a sardonic smile, this love was still toasting their feet.

'En we wensen u van hartig en zalig Kerstfeest,' said the priest, his Christmas blessing on the congregation and their cue to depart.

It wasn't hard to have hasty goodbyes with the parents who'd hosted a fine holiday eve feast. They would all see one another soon enough in the coming New Year. Until then, Ankie and Tinus promised to make a daily cycle to look in on the kittens, opting for that instead of taking them home for a week of getting lost in an unsettling new environment. After much thanks, it was for Femke's sake that Felly and Kieran rode immediately home so she could get a good night's rest before the morning's journey to Ireland. With everything packed and ready, theirs would be another quick Uber to the train station where they would meet up with Filip and Moira again to catch an early flight out of Schiphol Airport.

15

Christmas time in Ireland was a passion play of lights and good cheer, beginning at the airport after planes touched down and passengers walked into the varying terminals. This began with the 'welcome home, welcome to Ireland' greeting when passing through customs. Those indigenous to the country who were working and living abroad in other EU countries no longer had to exchange identifications. They were a recognised part of a union of 28 member states. EU citizens all stood in the same customs queues, and returning to their homeland more often than not would present them with a warmer greeting. The McNeela home would display a white candle in the window as well. Kieran's mother, Bridget, would not forget another old Irish tradition of natives keeping watch for their returning emigrated sons and daughters.

Felly likened the differences between Dutch and Irish celebrations as night and day, boiled potatoes and chips. Both in her mind were lovely. Albeit classy, the staider festivities of the Calvinistic country she was brought up in could appear duller in the eyes of those partaking in the jolly folly of a somewhat chaotic land, where many still believed in the existence of elves and fairies. Femke was in love with her Celtic roots and embraced everything with little guile. 'Good craic,' Kieran called it, and rightly so.

'We've tickets for a Christmas panto,' said Bridget, after embracing her children and hugging her granddaughter with an extra squeeze.

'A what?' said Felly.

'Kwistmas pants, Mama. Nana bought me kwistmas pants,' her voice not hiding her disappointment.

'Did ye buy her some Christmas pants?' asked Kieran, popping a Murphy's from the refrigerator and handing another to his wife.

Kieran's sister Sinead walked in on them, snickering as she held up a set of yellow Tayto Nation boxer shorts meant as a gag gift probably for herself. With a devilish look she presented them to Femke, whose mouth was dropping but was too polite to comment. Instead, she gave her mother a pleading look.

Kieran chuckled at the youngest in the sibling pecking order, him being second to last. 'Still up to tormenting children, I see, Sis.'

She smiled and hugged both him and Felly. 'I wouldn't have it any other way. So, what'd ye think, Muppet? Isn't yer granny's gift grand?'

'It's ugly,' blurted the child, almost in tears.

'I think yer aunt is taking the mickey. Mam? Please explain to yer granddaughter what a Christmas panto is.'

'Me too, please,' said Felly.

'Don't pay those two any mind, darlin'. We're going to see 'Cinderella'.'

Femke suddenly brightened, forgetting she had almost broken into tears. 'Oh, thank you, Nana.' Defiance in her voice. 'I hates ugly underpants.'

'Me too. Feckin' nephew, Collin, wrapped 'em up for me under the tree.' Sinead snickered again. 'Gaw, he knows how addicted I am to Taytos, though.'

Her brother winked at her. 'Salt and vinegar?'

'Only the best.'

Felly turned to Kieran's mother. 'So, what's a Christmas panto? Does this mean that the Cinderella story will be done in pantomime?

'Something like that. Lots of audience participation that encourages hissing and booing.'

'And loads of spittin'.'

Kieran nodded to his sister. 'So, bring a towel.'

'Sounds like fun, especially for children.'

'Oh, they love it so, adults too because it's all done in camp. Some of the themes go over the little ones' heads, but it's loads of craic.'

'Mammy wants to take the little mite and leave ye with some time for yerselves. Yer stayin' through Boxing Day, right?'

'We are and thanks. That's a nice Christmas present for us too.'

'Grand, it was the only day left for tickets.'

'That popular?

The blonde sister nodded her head. 'Unbelievably popular.'

'Well, that'll work out perfectly,' said Felly; 'and it's awfully sweet of you both.'

Kieran gave a nod to his sister. 'I don't know about sitting that one near our daughter, though.'

Sinead stood her ground. 'Well, I am a primary school teacher.'

'And God help all them mites.'

'Anyone for a cup of tea?' Bridget interjected. 'Food is on the table, buffet style. We've got a lot of it, so just tuck in.'

'I'm fine, thanks,' said Kieran.

'I'd love a cup,' said Felly. 'But if it's Lyons I'll be needing some milk in it.'

'Ah, go on,' the mother replied to her son. 'I'm making a cup for the both of ye. It's no problem a'tal.'

'I'm grand, Mam, really. I'm still nursing this beer.'

Their mother returned to the kitchen to put on the kettle as the others entered the large parlour with an even larger kitchen table, looking like all the extra table leaves had been inserted to stretch its length from wall to wall. Resting atop a green tablecloth was a hodgepodge of Pyrex dishes filled with assorted casseroles, a veritable potluck of meats, vegetables, cheese and sauces to choose from. To the side were a few Christmas cracker leftovers, most had been popped and discarded next to crumpled up party hats.

'I thought I heard familiar voices in here.' The eldest of the two older brothers came into the room, greeting Kieran with a handshake and Felly with a kiss on the cheek. 'Howeyeh?'

'Good, good, good. How's the construction business?'

James swelled his chest. 'Couldn't be better. And how's biz in the lowlands.'

'Can't complain either.'

He winked at Felly 'Has yer man been treatin' ye alright then?'

'Holding his own and doing his best to keep up with me.'

He laughed at that, looking at his younger brother. 'I'll bet he has. Ian just turned on the telly and found a game on RTE. Want to join us?'

Kieran lifted his beer to him. 'Do ye mind, darlin'?'

'Not at all. Go for it. I'll look in on your mother and see if she needs a hand with anything.'

'I'm sure she does, and don't take no for an answer.'

'I'll keep that in mind.' After being married to an Irishman all these years, Felly knew that an Irish 'no' was often just an invitation to be asked again, even insisting unless the other strongly opposed, which she didn't think Bridget would do.

'I didn't forget to add milk, Felicia.' Bridget presented her a chipped cup with pretty pink azaleas.

'Thanks. I actually prefer it over beer.'

'Not much of a drinker, are ye?'

'Wine mostly. I do prefer the reds, though I don't mind a dry Chardonnay or Riesling once in awhile.'

'Shall we then? I like a good Cabernet, myself.' She pulled an open bottle out of the fridge and poured them both a glass. 'Sláinte.'

'Sláinte mhath.'

'Near perfect, darlin'. I can see my son's been a good influence. So, how's things? Ye both look tired.'

'These past few months have been an admitted strain after the drowning of my colleague. Did Kieran tell you he's been representing the man who did it?'

'So, it was murder then?'

'You know about lawyer-client confidentiality, right? Kieran's good at keeping a tight lip.'

189

'He certainly doesn't get that from me,' she smirked. 'But I know my son admires the talent ye have for sleuthing.'

'Thank you for saying that. I often get the feeling my penchant for looking under rocks is just me being a pest.'

Bridget laughed loudly. 'If you were a man no one would dare think that of you. Just stand yer ground, girl. But, in my mind, yer greatest gift is the little mite who takes so much after her own mam.'

Felly eyed Kieran's mother lovingly just then. 'Everyone looks at Femke as Kieran's mini-me.'

'It's just the blonde hair. I see that curious mind of yours in her. And she's sharp as a whip with her Irish too. Whoever she takes after, ye've both done alright with that one.'

'Cheers.'

'Now tell me about this case.'

'Well, it started off like this....' And Felly spent the better part of the afternoon filling in her mother-in-law on all that had been happening that fall in Leiden and Den Bosch. 'First, I find this bead that the department secretary, Trudi Langmeijer, frets over, her body language alone giving her away. And, come to find out, she and Evi Anneveldt, the murder victim, were not only colleagues but also secondary schoolmates in Den Bosch. After I found this out it made sense to me why Evi wanted to talk to her. She'd been so anxious to tie up loose ends after getting the bad news that her cancer had spread. Trudi swears, though, that they hadn't been anywhere near the bridge, and I believed her when she said that Evi had just wanted a shoulder to cry on. So, they met in a local pub and tied one on together. Cancer is such a devasting disease.'

'Was that the only evidence, this bead? I wouldn't think much of it, myself.'

'It did lead me to Trudi, and later I paid her a follow-up visit, bringing Femke with me. Having a child with you just makes you seem less threatening, and Trudi warmed to her right away. We got to talking about families and our childhoods, which was when she showed me some of her old class photos. When I saw the Polaroid of her, Evi and Dirk together I felt I had my proof. I got so close to cracking the case with it, hoping your son would see it as a possible motive for a crime and not just an accident.'

'And did he?'

'He showed it to his client and then gave it back to me, saying he couldn't discuss the case.'

'That doesn't seem fair, but it sounds to me like he's caught, as we say in English, between a rock and a hard place.'

'If the guilty man has any scruples he'll confess.'

'You feel certain that yer man is guilty?'

'I do, Bridget. I feel it in my gut.'

She raised a brow. 'Unfortunately, guts don't convict. And this borrowed photograph is what Kieran took to yer man, Dirk? This is all getting too complicated for me. I still don't see how all this could provoke murder.'

'The baby Evi was carrying was the key. It turns out that Evi and Kieran's client were childhood sweethearts. And when she became pregnant, her family made the decision to hush everything up and put the baby up for adoption. I don't think Dirk even knew he had a son by her, which was a secret that Evi had kept for years until her terminal cancer overwhelmed her, spreading to her brain and kidney.'

'Oh my.'

'I can't blame her for not wanting to be buried with her secrets.'

'In my day they just sent unmarried women to the laundries.'

'I heard about those laundries.'

Bridget sadly nodded her head. 'A blight on our past of how women have been treated in this country.'

'And your history books never mentioned a thing about it, either?'

'Not a word, not a word,' she breathed out. 'But we girls shuddered at the thought of ever endin' up there.' Finishing her glass, she poured another and topped up Felly's. 'And it all ended with this long-lost son's beating?'

'Yes, poor Pascal. He did get the worst of it, but he seems to be handling everything quite maturely and moving on.'

'Perhaps it's harder for the older generations. Many of us haven't learnt to be as openly forgiving and accepting. I'm still working on this, myself.'

'You're a lovely woman, Bridget. Kieran's lucky to have you as his mam.' She smiled, then said, 'But when Pascal found out the very man who he'd had this dalliance with at a sauna ten years ago was his father, he was devastated.'

'And I'm sure the father was too.'

'Neither knew who each other was till recently, and I believe that Dirk Nolten just went into denial.'

'Sins of the fathers...and of the mothers too.'

She eyed the other woman sidewise. 'If you believe in

such a thing, yes.'

'What I believe is that we are role models to our children, and how we live our lives has a domino effect. Yet, what you're describing here reminds me of a Greek tragedy, a homophile 'Oedipus Rex.''

'You read Sophocles too?' Felly was impressed.

'They may not have openly discussed the laundries, but 'Oedipus Rex' was on every secondary school reading list.'

'Not on ours, not unless you were on a literature and linguistics trajectory like me.'

'So, what now? What's the next step?'

'There isn't any, I'm afraid...not unless we get a confession. And I say a big generic 'we'. Pascal told me he'd gone to visit his father before his release, telling me that confronting the man while he still behind bars was the safest way for him to do it. And, afterward, he decided not to press charges. He said this just gave him more peace of mind...considering the circumstances.'

'After giving him a piece of his, I'm sure.'

Felly smiled at that. 'I'm sure too. He no longer wants anything to do with the man.'

'It takes courage to confront one's demons, especially after they beat you to a pulp.'

'Kieran still thinks that Dirk has a good case, though he doesn't go into specifics with me. So, I have no idea what he means by it.'

'He's thinking he can prove the man's innocence, from the sound of it.'

'But how can he think that, Bridget? It just makes sense to me that he's not.'

'I know, I know, ye feel it in yer gut.'

Just then Femke skipped into the kitchen with the yellow Tayto boxer shorts on her head, giggling hysterically.

Both mother and grandmother laughed at the sight of her. Holly, another grandchild a few years older, rushed in after with her head covered up by boxer shorts that were decorated with lace. 'Another gag gift I believe our Holly's wearing,' said Bridget.

Then Holly said to her grandmother, 'We're putting on our own panto,'

Femke nodded her head furiously, a leg of the underwear falling past her nose. 'And I'm getting my knickers in a twist.'

The city of Dublin, where Nana Bridget was taking her granddaughters to the panto, has a notorious reputation for a vibrant nightlife of a majority youth culture known to get fairly ossified on gat and crisps. In other words, they were having their fair share of Guinness and curry cheese Taytos, as it was never too hard to 'go on the gargle, get pissed or truly wrecked' with over 668 licensed pubs to choose from. Designated drivers with the misfortune of drawing the short straw would have to have mineral water instead, especially with sobriety checkpoints along the road and the guards on patrol who were proving to be fierce. Like Amsterdam in the Netherlands, Dublin had earned its party town name. Yet, this fair city had so much more to offer, such as its highly rated universities like Trinity College and the Royal College of Surgeons. The historic buildings of O'Connell Street had also fascinating histories of uprisings and bloodshed rooted in the very foundations of the

Republic. And Temple Bar and other cultural quarters were popular centres as well for studio and performance venues, which was where Brigid McNeela and her girls were heading.

When the ladies left for their Cinderella pantomime, Felly and Kieran booked a room for the night at a resort hotel in the village of Sneem. 'Here be leprechauns,' said Felly when their borrowed Toyota approached the quaint little town.

'Just about,' said Kieran, 'but wait till ye see our hotel. Nothing for the fairies, I can guarantee.'

The N70, an Irish national roadway, passes through the town of Sneem (meaning 'knot' in Irish Gaelic), then meanders its way along the scenic Ring of Kerry before ending up in the heavily touristed city of Kilarney. The route cuts through lush mountains of grazing sheep and curves back upon breath-taking sea views, which can also be cycled if one is fit enough to take on the challenge of a strenuous climb. Most people travel by car or coach, which many touring buses now do. And the village of Sneem is a major tourist attraction because of its old-fashioned charm that can be seen in the colourfully painted buildings that house the local shops and pubs geared for the seasonal tourist trade that often passes through en masse, especially in the summer months. Where Sneem got its name was most likely geographical, it literally being split in two by the body of roaring water flowing into Kenmare Bay, in the estuary just below the town. It was also linked by a stone footbridge acting as a knot between the two north and south squares.

Felly only remembered the time they passed through on summer holiday on their way to visit the Robinson cousins who were then living in Kenmare. As they approached the village, Kieran suddenly stopped the car, laughing and pointing at a scruffy looking bearded man who was holding a leash with a dumbfounded expression. Felly looked out her window and saw another man in an electric wheelchair being chased by a big goat with a broken collar. The goat almost knocked over the poor old gentleman in its attempts to hijack an open box of dog biscuits he must have been feeding him. It looked to have broken free of its leash before appropriating the whole box and guzzling down its contents as the man's chair listed before up righting again. All this was happening as a busload of German tourists parked next to the scruffy man watched agape, some even capturing the scene on camera rather than lending a helping hand.

'Probably being uploaded on YouTube as we watch,' laughed Kieran, who then nonchalantly turned the key to the engine and drove off.

On this day, Kieran bypassed the town and turned onto a very long drive with lush green all around. The hotel atop the hill looked to Felly like a hunting lodge that was tucked away on well-kept grounds, and it overwhelmed her with its beauty. Their transport was on loan from Kieran's eldest sister, Grace, who, with her husband and two children, had left that morning for Spain. Parking was free onsite, and the owner's friendly Irish Setter, named Red, was there to greet them. To Felly, having a Setter greet you on your travels was always a good sign, and she got out and pet the happy dog. The suite Kieran had booked for them was above ground level and overlooked a lake, or what was really a body of brackish water that flowed in from the River Sneem. Their view was breathtaking, and they both couldn't wait to explore the grounds. First things first, though. Their long overdue tryst took priority and demanded no interruptions.

Kieran was still rifling through his pack, grinning, as Felly pulled back the covers and slid in bed. 'Whatever are you doing?' she said.

'Looking for my box of Roses.'

'Your what?'

'I knew I hadn't forgot to pack it.' He handed her the Cadbury Roses chocolates and said, 'I would have splurged on a real bouquet but I feared it would have wilted on the way.'

'Why, they're lovely. Come here, you. You with your chocolates.' She undressed him with her eyes as he literally undressed. Then he climbed in, kissing her gently on her neck. 'What was I thinking? Forget the bloody chocolates,' he said, breathing into her ear. 'Ah, but isn't this grand? I've almost forgotten what it feels like.'

'Yes,' she purred. 'No interruptions. Just pure unadulterated sex.'

And they made love with their curtains open wide and nothing out the window but rolling hills and open sky. Winter weather was creeping in, the air crisp and crackling outside but the heating was turned up within. Along with the strong stream of sunlight on their bodies, they were toasting deliciously as they slowly swayed from side to side, linked to familiar rhythms as each entered the other like two spoons melting. Softly melting, one into the other.

They remained in bed till dusk, forgetting to take their walk along the grounds. It was such a delightful feeling, the tussled bed, the sweet smell of sweat glazing their bodies. Should they order room service? Break into the minibar? Linger a little longer while feeding each other chocolates?

197

With a kiss and a bit from the box of roses, they grinned happily at their decadence. 'Shall we live here forever?'

'Let's do, yes.'

They heard music playing in the bar and dining area below, which intrigued them. They rose languidly and gracefully, their tempo unhurried. And they only moved to play in the shower, like youth half their ages. Squeaky-clean they were, their fingers all wrinkled. Kieran stepped out first and towel-dried his hair. Then he threw his towel at her and she ducked, laughing and sticking out her tongue at him. They dressed warmly in their jeans and Aran sweaters, which had been given them as Christmas gifts. Then they headed down to the bar area and found a vacant table, ordering drinks and dinner as they listened to the guitar player still there. He was now taking requests. 'Just not 'Here comes Santa Claus',' he said. 'He's come already. Hasn't he, boys and girls?'

Kieran blurted out. 'He sure has.'

'Oh, stop,' said Felly, grinning as her face coloured.

The musician looked their way and, to Felly's embarrassment, winked at them. He began playing and singing, 'Santa Baby', as patrons groaned and laughed.

Felly had put in an order for cider this time, and Kieran a pint of Guinness. When their drinks came, they lifted their glasses to the guitarist. He smiled at them in return. Then he gazed out the huge windows with glass doors leading to an outside deck. 'Look everyone, it's snowing. 'Let it snow, let it snow, let it snow', he sang. Patrons glimpsed where he was looking, watching the snowflakes as they drifted down and sailed alongside the windows like sparkling crystals in the air. They sipped their drinks when they appeared and watched along with the rest. 'Truly magical, isn't it?' said Kieran, his voice soft and dreamlike.

'Do you miss all this, babe?'

He took her ringed hand and kissed it. 'I wouldn't be lying if I said, yes.'

'Well, we don't always have to stay in Holland.'

'I know that, darlin'. Shall we retire here then?'

'Here? Now? In Sneem?' She was smiling at him.

He winked back at her and drank his pint, thinking that Guinness only tasted like Guinness in Ireland. He would order it nowhere else. 'To us, mo stór.'

'To us, lieverd,' she replied.

16

Back in Den Bosch, Dirk Nolten was inspecting his ageing hands, a workman's hands he had used to build up his business from nothing. He had always been good with his hands and was a risktaker, he thought. He would step out on the rim and would look up and out at the vast horizon, the nothingness before him as he took that step, that one small step, which was followed by another and another. He would get up if knocked down. Then he would start again. That's how you dared to build a company, he thought. And his was thriving. He hadn't shied from his proclivities either. Nor did he blame anyone else. Perhaps his were twisted. He only knew that sometimes what he did had gone against the grain. When you're twisted,' he had once heard an old alcoholic friend say, 'your head spins and you feel like screaming.' And now he was screaming, screaming inside. *Potverdorie*, and damn it to hell! Some of what he did, he did in secret, not so much because he was ashamed. He had long ago come to grips with who he was and what he did. He had never tried to rub it in anyone else's face, including his wife's. He loved her, but she wasn't enough. Did she know this? He was never sure. He thought she might have known, might have suspected all along, but chose to look the other way. Would she forgive him now? He didn't know that either. What he did, realising what he had done with his son Pascal, had crossed a line, even for him, though it had been unknowingly. Talk about twist! A twist in fate, damnable fate. His head was hurting. An ocular migraine was unwinding his head, unwinding his soul.

There was a chill in the air when Dirk had returned home from the station, a chill outside from oncoming winter, a chill inside from the icy reception at home. He could feel it plainly, knife-like, disagreeably cold and heart-stabbing. His soul was bleeding, and now his head. His wife had gone out. She had been long retired but still liked to volunteer her services at the blood blank. His daughter was rollerblading with friends. She was so innocent still and the only one who had greeted him with a smile. His son had come and gone, busy now with his own life and his friends. Dirk was alone today and hitting the Scotch. He preferred it over his countrymen's inclination for gin, which was a 16th century Dutch invention that began as herbal medicine sold by local chemists. Scotch, to him, was a serious drinking man's drink. And he loved to get his hands dirty, his working hands, as he was a drinking man who loved his drink smooth and neat. He had a glass with him now. Too many shots had been consumed already to smell that aromatic barley he loved so well. The smell of man, he thought, the smell of himself.

Why Dirk's life had suddenly made such a twist and turn he felt had to do with that eccentric old bitch. He wasn't an insensitive man and pitied anyone who had cancer. Evi's plight had been a horrible infliction. But why in God's name had she felt that it gave her the right to upend his? He didn't have cancer, but she made his life one too, a malignant tumour exposed, or so he felt. Had he killed her? He hadn't thought so. They had argued, yes, over what he couldn't believe she was telling him. After all those years, to have kept such a secret from him he felt was utterly cruel and insensitive. Bitch. The two of them had completely lost touch over the years. But what a couple they had been at their VWO, the gymnasium, or six-year preparatory school before university. They had been voted the couple of the year by their schoolmates. Oh, happy days was their young and innocent world that was wide open with possibilities. He had no clue then that she had become pregnant. It must have been their senior year, which was when she had suddenly disappeared from his life. She was there with him one day and gone the next. That had been a slap in the face, and a further insult when the family began refusing his calls. There were also his letters that had returned to him unopened. Heartless. And all his efforts were dashed when doing his best to get in touch with her. He still remembered wondering at the time what he had done for her to have left him like that? Without a word or an explanation. Only what he thought had mattered so much one day had mattered nothing at all the next.

So, Dirk was surprised when Evi had suddenly reached out to him. Was it only this past month? It seemed like eons ago. And when she called, he could tell she was drunk. Maybe strung-out on drugs even? She pled with him, insisting that he meet up with her. Then she divulged the news about her cancer and how it was spreading while apologising for the urgency of the call. She had a secret to share. And this, she told him, she no longer wanted to bear alone.

Evi never knew of Dirk's bisexuality, which he had only come to grips with as he grew in age and knowledge of life and himself in it. She was certainly unaware of the fling he had with Pascal at the Hague's Blue River Sauna. Back in the day, the youth he had flirted with was not much older than his son, Reinier. And neither knew then that they were related, father and son. What dark irony, the radical differences of how life was expected to unfold, more strangely true than fiction. And there were many of them. Now he was faced with this shame, thanks to the Pandora's box of Evi. But he hadn't killed her. He had wanted to, and perhaps his baser self could have easily wrung her neck. Oh, the two of them had argued and raged. Such were their mutual tempers. She shoved him and he shoved back, even slapping her to the ground, tipsy drunk and crying. She disgusted him. And he turned from her. When he got in his car he sat there for awhile, his hands shaking while he gripped the wheel. As he turned the key to the ignition, he thought he heard a splash. He no longer cared and drove home blinded by his own tears, alone and outraged.

Dirk hadn't killed Evi, but could he have prevented her death? Now he felt dead inside while aware of something heroic he might have done but did not do. He was a coward after all, left vulnerable to his own fate. His wife knew too. After picking him up at the police station, she demanded an explanation. His son, Reinier, knew only so much, knowing that he had a brother. Only the wife knew all of what he had confessed to her at his return. And she took everything in as she always seemed to do, bearing his burden in her cool acceptance. She kissed him then on the cheek, and then she removed herself from his presence. Can you kiss and kill with kindness? Hers was deafening, smothering. He couldn't deny the ambivalence he detected in her eyes, the deadpan in her voice. He was glad when she left him for the blood bank. Glad to be alone now in his self-loathing.

Dirk stopped inspecting his hands. He put on his jacket and grabbed his car keys then drove to the tracks, climbed the fence and leapt onto the rails.

It was Reinier's mother who found the letter from Dirk. 'Dear Family,' it read. 'I need to confess my shame and inability to be all I have wanted to be for you. Please don't blame Pascal either. Neither of us knew who each other was back when we were just having a bit of fun. He was so young too, like a flirtatious teen trying on costumes in a clothing shop. Nothing more. I'm not excusing our behaviour, especially mine. I also admit that Pascal wasn't the respectable professor you see now.'

Dirk added how he regretted his own actions but could not be anything more, or anyone else, than who he really was, which he sincerely hoped they would eventually come to understand. If not, or they would not, he was sorry for that too and sad that he had not been a better man.

'To you, Jenny, my wife, my love,' wrote Dirk. 'Pity me for not having the strength to tell you this to your face. And, Reinier, forgive me, son. I have no excuse for wanting to compensate my lack with such overbearing behaviour. Rinske, too, I hope that you will always know how much I have loved and cherished you.'

This was the contents of what Jenny had found and opened on their bed that day when she had come home from offering her services at the blood bank. And after she read it she cried out in great sobs.

The service for Dirk was short, raw and tender, ending with a sweet but sombre message of remembrance to all those mourners who had shown up in black to pay polite attention to an employer, colleague, client and friend. The Nolten family displayed little more than bewilderment on all their faces. And those involved in the suicide, such as the train's machinist and conductor, would need time off for trauma counselling. Passengers too would grumble and shake their heads for the inconvenience and sheer stupidity of such a senseless act of jumping in front of their train.

Jenny Nolten had emailed Dirk's attorney, Kieran McNeela, asking if he would attend the memorial service and stay afterward to discuss certain legalities regarding the wrapping up of her husband's case file. Felly, who had been their son Reinier's university professor, had accompanied her husband on the short flyover to Eindhoven Airport, where they then could take a train only minutes away from Den Bosch.

As the service concluded, a very troubled looking ex-student sought out his professor and asked if she wouldn't mind walking with him onto the mortuary's veranda.

'You'll catch your death of cold,' said Felly. 'The weather's sharp outside.'

'Please indulge me, Professor. I need to talk, and in private.'

'All right. Best to take your coat then.'

Reinier grabbed the grey corduroy jacket he had left on one of the chairs and followed her out. 'Mind if I smoke?'

'I didn't know that you did. When did you start that up?'

'Only recently,' he said, speaking with some discomfort. 'It calms the nerves.'

She eyed the pain in his eyes, so wanting to hug him like a child and repeat words of placating comfort, such as 'grief is like an ocean', and 'this too shall pass'. Yet this was no child beside her, and neither would hugs be appropriate nor empty words soothe. 'I'm listening, Reinier,' she said, instead. 'Whenever you're ready.'

He took a drag on his lit cigarette and exhaled. 'I'd followed my father that night he met with Professor Anneveldt by the bridge.'

She blinked once, swallowing hard in an attempt not to look too surprised. 'You did? How did that come about? I saw you in class the morning after.'

'I often go home at the weekend. It's less than an hour and a half away by train. You know that.' He eyed her directly and she nodded her head. Then he continued. 'All my life I've been trying to figure out the man who's been such an enigma to me. A successful businessman, but one rarely present. And he wasn't the greatest father when he was. I know he cared for us; and in his letter, I think he'd done his limited best to tell us so. Let's face it, the man was good with his hands but not so good with his emotions. It all makes sense to me now; I mean, him being gay.'

She digested what he was saying as she stood against the cold exterior wall, weighing her words. 'I don't think he was, though...gay, I mean. He appeared to love your mother very much. You and your sister as well.'

Reinier spat out, 'He was a dominating bastard, you mean?' He took another puff, letting it slowly fill his lungs. 'I wouldn't call what he did love, it was more like serving his own needs. We were just on the side, the family making him look complete. Anyway, he'd been acting more strange than usual that night, and I guess I just wanted to know what was up. I'm pretty fast on my bike. So, it wasn't hard for me to keep up as I pedalled fast and rode behind his car. I know he never saw me. Otherwise, he would have pulled over but never did. He drove straight on to the quayside, to the bridge and parked. Then he got out and walked down the embankment. I left my bike beside an SUV a few cars down and quietly went over to where he was on the knoll beneath me. It was then I saw the figure of a woman, thinking Dad was having an affair. Now I wanted to eavesdrop. This was crazy.' He stopped, inhaling smoke. 'Even crazier was when I recognised the anthropology professor from LU. I mean, what? I couldn't believe my eyes. I was on my belly now, and the grass was so wet. But what did I care at this point? I mean, my dad chatting her up like they were long lost friends?'

'I heard that they had been, actually.'

'Yeah? Well, that was the first time I heard anything about it. It was like watching some bad flick play out, like a midnight B-movie. I couldn't catch much of what they were saying, not until they got nasty and starting yelling at each other. Then I could hear them both loud and clear.'

'And what were they saying?'

'That crazy ass bitch was telling Dad they had a son together. This was evidently news to him too because, well, because he said so.'

'And what was your father doing all this time?'

He lowered a brow. 'What do you mean? They were both just standing there.'

'I mean, did he get violent with her?'

'No, not at first. Like I said, he was just standing there like in a stupor, I mean, when he wasn't yelling at her. So, she said that he had got her pregnant in their teens.

Then he called her a liar. But she insisted that she wasn't lying. She was saying that it was her family who'd forced her to drop out of school. Then when the kid was born, they immediately gave it up for adoption. My father then asked her why she was lying to him.'

Felly sighed. 'I could imagine his shock.'

'Well, he did ask if what she was saying was true then why had she waited so long to tell him. I mean, it's really kickass to know Pascal's my half-brother, but the dude's now 29 years old. What the ...? None of this made sense. And Professor Anneveldt? She was looking wasted to me, wobbling around like she was high on something.'

'I believe it was Oxycodone mixing with whatever alcohol she'd consumed earlier.'

'No shit? How do you know all this? Were you with her earlier too?'

'No, I didn't really know her. It was a friend who told me this.'

He shook his head back and forth. 'That's messed up.'

'This was no place you should have been, Reinier. You should have gone home and maybe confronted your father afterward about all this. If nothing else, at least to get your story straight. He should have had this conversation with you, instead of you now having it out with me. But what a nightmare for you.'

'Yeah, well, it was.'

'So, did you leave then? Did they see you?'

'No, I felt frozen in place, like I couldn't move. They were oblivious to me and started yelling at each other again. I saw her get in his face and shove him in anger. He lost his cool, shoving her and slapping her back. Then she was down on her knees, sobbing. It was pathetic. The two of them.'

'Oh my God, yes. Still, it's no excuse for shoving and slapping a woman.'

'Yeah, I know, even though she shoved him first. And you and I both know that Dad's got a temper.'

Felly only sighed.

'Anyway, it was then I saw him reach down to her. I think he even said he was sorry, but I could have been mistaken because their voices suddenly got quieter. I did hear her say, though, that it was no use...something like that.'

She sighed, shaking her head. 'So, then what happened?'

'That was when she dropped the bomb on Dad, telling him she had stage four cancer and was dying. She said she no longer wanted to keep her secrets. She didn't want to take them to the grave.'

'And your dad?'

'How did Dad react, you mean? Well, he wasn't happy. He turned around and left.'

'He just left?'

'That's what I said.' Reinier took a last drag on the butt of his cigarette. 'It wasn't Dad who killed her, Felly. It was me.'

'What? No, you didn't.' She shook her head in disbelief. 'Don't say that.'

'But I did. Dad took off and I went down and shoved her in the water. I didn't know she hit her head along the way. I just wanted to hurt her. Then I too turned around and walked away...like my chickenshit dad.'

Felly was trying to process everything quickly, wondering what to do next.

'All I was thinking then was that this bitch was going to ruin our family. She was certainly hurting my dad.'

'Oh my, oh my. So, what do you want to do now?'

'I want to turn myself in. Will your husband help me?'

'Let's go find out,' she said sadly.

Kieran spoke at length with Felly's distraught ex-student, advising him to do the right thing. 'It'll work out better in the long run if ye do. Felly and I will be there too,' he assured. 'But first, would ye consider giving yer mam the courtesy of an explanation? She really shouldn't be left out of the loop.'

Chagrined, Reinier nodded his head, saying that he would.

'We'll be staying another night at our hotel. Just have the front desk page us when yer ready, and we'll all ride to the station together.'

Kieran called a cab at Reinier's return, and Felly went along with them in support but remained in the waiting room as they were ushered in to be interviewed, Kieran acting as Reinier's legal counsellor. When taken to a holding cell, the young man blinked twice and took a deep breath, attempting not to panic. Kieran told him then that he and Felly would be returning to Ireland for the remainder of their holidays. He promised, however, that he would be back to counsel him further before his upcoming court date.

17

After their return to Cork, it was Felly and Kieran's plan to spend the remainder of their time in Ireland with her twin, his wife and the Robinson cousins in County Kerry. So, they hugged the mam and headed up the coast. Aidan and Sean had continued to work for the Irish Coast Guard after the sale of Taisce, the farmhouse that they and Moira had inherited. With their split proceeds, the two men pooled funds together and bought a small condominium in Dingel, a quaint harbour town and home to the legendary dolphin, Fungi. According to the lads, theirs was a roomy enough dwelling, and they'd been more than satisfied with the investment. Yet, the space now occupied was exacerbated by the pop-in guests and verging on the brink of cosy disaster. Femke, though, had scoped out a beanbag chair to plop into. And with her iPad and the treats that Moira had the foresight to purchase and stock on the masculine metal kitchen shelves before their arrival, she managed to make herself at home.

While in Dingel, they all mostly hung out together, drinking and watching TV sports for the remainder of their stay. Felly and Moira were able to escape for frequent walks, though. Femke was with them on one of their quayside meanderings, because this day they were on the lookout for that notorious old dolphin.

'Surely Fungi's dead by now,' whispered Felly to Moira, both scanning the horizon of the sea. 'How long do dolphins live, anyway?'

'Gaw, Fungi's a god. He's gonna live forever.' Moira winked at Femke. 'What do ye think, muppet? Do ye see the auld flipper?'

The little girl hadn't responded, seemingly engrossed in the rocks and shells she'd been picking up along the way. She smiled up at them once before returning to what she was doing, singing softly. 'When will that spesho someone sweep me off my feet?'

Felly laughed out loud. 'Where did you hear that from?'

Femke was caught off-guard. 'What?'

'That song you were singing. About that special someone to sweep you off your feet?'

She distractedly kicked at a black pebble. 'Cinderella's a princess, Mama.

'Oh, you were singing about Cinderella. Would you like to be a princess too, poppie?'

'No, I'm fine. Can I pet Fungi if he swims up to us?'

Both women chuckled, Moira's eyes were transfixed on the ocean waves as she said, 'Fungi probably swam out to mind all them baby dolphins at his cave home.'

The little girl pouted. 'So, he's not coming back.' Then she returned to her singing. 'That spesho someone....'

Felly turned to Moira just then. 'It'll be sad leaving Ireland, but I'll be glad to get back home, just the same. I've a lot of preparation to do before next semester's courses begin. Did I tell you they're letting me teach a class in rhetoric this term? I'm quite excited about that.'

'I miss the cats too,' Femke interjected.

'Ah, Ireland, yer in me bones.' Moira was still gazing in the distance as she said: 'Oh, I long for the shores, of the land not distant from her people. An abandoned mother the soul leaves behind.'

'That sounds like a poem,' said Felly. 'Are you quoting someone?'

'I am. An unknown poet from my childhood. I love her words so.'

'Any more to it?'

She nodded, continuing. 'And her black green Cliffs of Moher are aproning the seagulls circling round and round.'

'Beautiful.'

Femke stopped picking up shells as she also listened to Moira's hypnotic cadence.

'Her heathered fields of gorse brown gold and walk-whistling lads with Gaelic tongue.' The sister-in-law squeezed her eyes, adding, 'The devil take their mother's soul, though they'll toast her when the workday's done.'

'Good lads.' Felly laughed.

'Ach, yeah. 'Come court me with another round, boys, while we still have our heads about us. Cream-crested stout and peat brown ale where neither craic nor ceol confound us."

'What is 'ceol'?

'That's Irish for music, craic agus ceol. It's just fun and music.'

'So, why would fun music be confounding?'

'I think she means it as a double-entendre, like such fun really wouldn't be so overwhelmin'. Or maybe so. Yet it's still worth the price. Like Yeats and his 'everything that's lovely is but a brief, dreamy, kind delight'.'

'I love the way the Irish look at life, like a mystery ready to unfold, not typically obvious and never to be taken for granted. Your language too, it's so full of rich connotations.'

'I don't know about that,' laughed Moira. 'It's all just plain Irish to me.'

'And it does sound like your poet appreciated the finer things in life.'

'Ach, yeah, she did that. And she always gets me cravin' a gat.'

'Of course, your word for Guinness, right? Well, let's go have one then. I see a pub nearby.'

Everything that occurred when they returned to the Netherlands was like a domino effect of cascading events. The fate of the Nolten family at the new year's beginning was a sad one while they struggled to recover from the husband and father's suicide. Jenny Nolten no longer volunteered at the local blood bank. For days she would lie in bed, watching television with a wet cloth pressed to her forehead. Her son and daughter coped by doing light household chores and cooking meagre dinners. A menu of macaroni and cheese was their staple. Occasionally, they would get their mother to sit with them for the evening meal. Rinske would run a comb through Jenny's unkempt hair and help her into the kitchen as she lowered her tired body into a chair. She never ate much but would mostly stare at the plate set before her and sigh. It was Reinier who had finally put an end to this behaviour by dragging the moaning and groaning woman to the shower room with the demand that she clean up and dress. 'I've got in touch with a social worker, and she's coming over today,' he said. 'The appointment is at two o'clock. So, pull yourself together, Mom, please.'

On the day of Reinier's court case, Kieran was present and at his side, though unable to sit with him directly during the proceedings. Felly was seated in the visitor section next to Reinier's mother. The elder woman had been helped by her social worker to make herself presentable for her son's court date. Reinier's sister, Rinske, was too young to be allowed to sit in court with them, and the social worker agreed to spend the morning making friendship bracelets with her while her mother and brother were away. As the proceeding began, the court's sitting and standing magistrates entered from different chambers. Judge Janssen appeared dressed in a black robe with white band, and she went over to the middle of a raised elongated table where she sat and opened the file before her. The prosecutor, Meester Bakker, walked over and stood at the dais directly facing her.

Theatrics are not typically displayed in the Dutch court of law. The magistrates are seen as acting representatives of the legal system rather than elevated persons of power for sentencing others. Today's judge spoke as soon as she seated herself, making plain her objective to be as clear with this case as possible. 'I have prepared my thoughts on the basis of the facts accumulated in this police report before me,' she said, 'all of which was contained in the defendant's interview at the police station.' She motioned for the prosecutor and conferred with him while hearing his intent to convince her that Reinier's case was worthy of conviction. Kieran stepped up just then and presented his defence of death by misadventure. 'The push,' he said, 'was not the cause of death. It was an action done in a moment of anger that led to the fall. The victim hit her head only afterward, when she stumbled and went into the water. This injury, I want to point out, is something that my client was not aware of. And when he was, he turned himself in to the police and confessed his actions to them on his own accord.'

The judge nodded her head, looking again to Bakker, who pointed out different aspects of the report and pressed her for some indication of what the law should be. Reinier was then addressed by Judge Janssen who asked him to briefly state the series of events leading to his actions.

Reinier repeated what he thought were relevant bits and pieces of his dad and Evi's argument, how she had yelled at and threatened him before he shoved and slapped her then walked off. Neither Dirk nor Evi had seen Reinier before he went down to her. He didn't know why he did it, either. 'I was just so angry,' he said. 'And I'm sorry I pushed her.' There were tears in his eyes. He was doing his best to hold them back while repeating, 'I am so very sorry.'

The judge leaned over to him then. 'Yet, you did not come to her aid when she fell in the water. Why was that?'

Reinier shrugged his shoulders, looking to the floor with no answer.

'If doing nothing else, you could have at least called for help.'

'I didn't know she'd hit her head when I left. I just thought she was riled up and acting crazy.'

'The fact that you did not attempt to help her makes you guilty of direct influence. You initiated the whole thing by the push, and you did not respond properly when you heard the splash.'

'But, your honour, I really thought she could manage. The water may be four metres deep in that part of the canal, but I've swum it, myself, many times as a kid. I just didn't think it was all that dangerous.'

Judge Janssen looked at him sternly then rubbed her eyes before returning her attentions to the attorneys involved in the case. 'Help me out here. I want to take into account the actions of this young man.'

Kieran thought this a good moment to reiterate his thoughts. 'Reinier should not be held responsible for a gut reaction, and the push was a human reaction to his anger. This in itself is not a crime. Neither did Reinier initially intend for Evi Anneveldt to drown. He did not premeditate the action which would cause her to stumble and fall. He was not even aware that she hit her head when she went into the water. To him, her behaviour was merely 'erratic.' It was not his intention to kill her. He just pushed her out of anger.'

'I would agree that I do not see this action as a crime, itself,' said the judge.

Bakker weighed in at this point. 'Was the defendant's intent to cause the event? I do not think so either. He may not have had control over the development of the situation, but he was certainly the initiator. He has also made it clear to the court that he did not look back over his shoulder after hearing the splash. He did not act upon the situation but simply walked away.'

Janssen added, 'Even though he was angry, he should not have pushed the woman, which led to her stumbling and falling into the water. Nor did he take into account the life-threatening situation that happened to her afterwards. As he said of his own volition, he walked away.'

While seeking the right definition of the case's entirety and then putting it against the matrix of Dutch law, Judge Janssen found Reinier Nolten guilty of initiating the accident but not being able to control the death based on other factors beyond the situation. She reiterated that he had initiated the whole thing and had not properly reacted when hearing the splash. 'You could have also called the emergency number, which you did not do,' she said. 'And, thus, you are guilty of grievous bodily harm by failing in responsibility to help Evi Anneveldt out of the water.'

The court session concluded by sentencing Reinier to two years in prison for the way he hadn't taken personal responsibility. Afterwards, he would serve a five-year probation while attending an obligatory anger management course.

'We have considered your state of mind, and that you were angry,' said Judge Janssen. 'Yet, you are responsible for what you did and for the consequences of your actions. Your counsellor,' she added, motioning to Kieran, 'points out that you need to finish your schooling, as this will be affecting your whole life. So, you will be allowed to receive your degree before spending time in a prison facility for your crime.'

Reinier was none too happy about serving jail time, but he was glad to have confessed his terrible burden of guilt and felt a great weight had lifted from him. Thanks to Kieran's persuading the magistrates, he would also be able to finish his university studies. Nor did he mind the obligatory anger management courses, as he didn't want to end up like his dad, alone, misunderstood and unaccepting of himself. Minke promised that she would stand by him as well, and he proposed marriage to her then and there. Yet, she turned him down.

'I'd rather go into partnership together with an idea I have for an animal rescue foundation. What do you think?' She was grinning. 'We could call it 'All Things Barking Beautiful'.'

This took him back a moment, but Minke wasn't completely rejecting him. She didn't want marriage. She wanted to be his associate. 'So, the carat ring will be replaced by edible carrots?'

She laughed at that. 'Only if we raise rabbits.'

'You know.... I just had a thought, and I don't want to get ahead of myself here because I haven't even started my anger management courses. But why not rescue animals we could then train as therapy dogs? They could help people like me with their anger issues. Still, there's probably not a whole lot of profit in that.'

She shrugged. 'Probably not, but I can see a need for it just the same.'

'We'll just have to take these things a step at a time, then look for opportunities as they present themselves. First thing first is my dealing with this court sentence and finishing school. I'm seriously not looking forward to my time in jail, but it could have been worse.'

'Yes, it could have,' she agreed.

'And who knows? Maybe after all this I'll be able to go on to graduate school. I think then I'd want to specialise in something like behavioural finance.'

'Behavioural finance? I've never heard of that before. What is it?'

'I've just been reading up on it and find it interesting. It has something to do with how the financial beliefs we grow up with influence our decision-making later on. I'm gathering that it's kind of like a financial coaching degree, where the more we understand how we tend to invest ourselves the better choices we'll make.'

'That could be applied to anything, not just business.'

'Yeah, it could. But I'm just sticking with the basic finance track I'm on until getting my bachelor's. Then I'll work out the rest of my life from there.'

'Me too, but my degree is in clinical psychology.'

'Seriously? I thought you were an IT person.'

'Well, sort of. They do go together, you know. I've always been more interested in how people tick...in the head, not on the keyboard.'

He laughed. 'You really are an adorable dork.'

'I know. So, you want to go find a drink somewhere.'

Reinier eyed his wrist as if he were wearing a watch and said, 'Oh yeah. It's drink-o-clock.'

Minke laughed with him. 'Now who's the dork?'

18

Reinier's sister, Rinske, couldn't shake the anxiety she felt after her father's suicide. She was old enough to understand some of the pain of the man she had looked up to all her life, but she didn't know why exactly he had taken his, especially how he chose to end it so dramatically. There were nights when she had awakened in a cold sweat. Though almost in her teens, she cried out for her mother like a child of preschool age. Her secure world was gone and her life just felt darker these days.

At the suggestion of the social worker still visiting them, Jenny decided to take her daughter on holiday. She had always wanted to visit Copenhagen, and it was there that the two of them would go while waiting for Reinier to return to university. She booked a flight on a Scandinavian airline, and after checking in at their air B&B, they ventured off to see the famous statue of the 'Little Mermaid'.

'It's so small,' Rinske told her mother.

Jenny disappointedly agreed, but she liked seeing her daughter laughing. 'What next? Shall we go on some of the rides at Tivoli Gardens?'

The sad-eyed girl whispered to her mother. 'I'd rather go watch the fish swimming in the aquarium.'

'We can do that, yes. It's not far. We'll take a bus.'

The Danish transport system was efficiently easy for visitors to use, and Jenny soon realised that all she wanted to do could be done with her debit card. The national aquarium that the Danes called Den Blå Planet was located in Copenhagen's suburban city, Kastrup. And, to her, the building looked architecturally like a steel whirlwind resting atop water. She couldn't help but marvel at its cold but unique looking beauty. Rinske loved walking within the aquarium's promenade, and she stared into the walled glass of sea creatures. She could reach up and pretend she was touching the friendly manatees and feel like she was petting the Manta Rays as they flapped their fins like the wings of birds that were gently flying by. Even the sharks at feeding time didn't bother her. So much blood, but metres beyond her. She was shielded by glass and this felt safe. 'Mother, shall we go now?' she said suddenly. 'I'm hungry and I want to try the smorrebrod.'

Jenny nodded her head, and they left the aquarium, heading for the costly but picturesque town of Nyenhavn. There they would try their pick of open-faced sandwiches, such as the breaded fish filet or shrimp which was typically served on dark rye bread that was slathered with butter or lard. Jenny liked them all but decided on a simple egg and radish sandwich topped with lettuce that she could wash down with beer.

Rinske bit into her sandwich of roast beef with pickles and cheese while scanning the colourfully painted rowhouses along the harbour. 'I like Denmark. Maybe I'll study here someday. Do you think I could become a marine biologist, Mama?'

'I think you can become anything you want to be, schat. Anything, if you put your mind to it. And we have the funds. Your father left us a nice inheritance.'

'At least he did something right,'

'Try not to judge him too harshly, Rinske. Your papa did a lot of things right.'

She suddenly broke down and cried, the food she was swallowing tasted acrid like foil in her mouth. 'Then why did he jump in front of a train?'

Her mother shook her head, tears in her own eyes. 'He was a troubled man, but I know that he loved us...all of us.'

'Even his other son?'

'I suppose he did, yes.' There was pain in her eyes, her jaw setting. 'Even his other son.'

Pascal admitted to Xander how he had felt nothing for Dirk having taken his own life. Thoughts of his father left him blank, as any personal encounter, other than the recent beating and prison chat, had been so long ago. The shock of them being related would never completely leave him; this he knew and reckoned with. Mostly, he felt sorry for the family that Dirk had left behind in his cowardice. It was a strange feeling to be around Reinier now that he knew the two of them were related. Half-brothers. He somehow couldn't wrap his brain around that, admitting he was more comfortable leaving as much space as possible between them. He didn't need or want any further contact with the family, especially now that Reinier was aware of the intimacy he once shared with his dad, their dad. This casual, youthful fling of his while coming out. Why did it have to have been with his own father? 'Sick,' he muttered under his breath. 'Just sick.'

'What was that?' said Xander. He was busy trying out the new Fitbit he had bought online, laughing more than exercising. 'You really should try this,' he said. 'I'm almost getting the hang of it.'

'I think I'll pass. I'd rather run off my calories.'

Still laughing. 'You don't know what you're missing, man.'

'I think I do. Do you think I'm boring, Xander?'

He stopped exercising and looked at him. 'Why would you say that?'

'I don't know. Just a feeling I have, a dead feeling. Maybe we should try walking the Camino De Santiago in Spain. It sounds like a good time. And I think we're both fit enough to handle it.'

'Isn't that some kind of Catholic pilgrimage? I'm not that religious.'

'No, it's nothing like that. One of the anthropology professors I know does it every year. I think she's a Buddhist.'

'Sure then. We could look into that. I've always liked Spain, anyway. And wouldn't some of that warm sun on your face feel nice right now?'

'Ah, yes, yes it would. And the people you meet en-route? I think that's all part of the experience.'

'How's that?'

'Sharing bandages. Maybe swapping drinks and snacks along the way...and sharing stories too, I'd imagine.'

'Yeah, everyone has a story, don't they? We social animals aren't all that different when it comes right down to it.'

'Some more than most,' Pascal smirked.

Xander eyed his partner, taking in the handsomely squared jaw and stubbled beard. 'Well, not everyone can be a Pascal.'

'Only God could help them if they were.'

'Speaking of, not God, but help. I was talking to someone at work the other day.'

'Oh, here we go.'

'No, it's not like that. Hear me out on this. Marieke was telling me about a support group at the Erasmus clinic that deals with couples who've faced some trauma in their lives and are trying to build back their relationships.'

'Don't tell me you've been gossiping about us at the medical centre.'

'She only knows about us renewing our relationship and me wanting to work on keeping it together. You met her once at a BBQ in the park. You probably don't remember her, but she remembers you. She thought you were handsome.' He smiled, and Pascal noticed there was love in his soft brown eyes. 'She also knows you've been going through some personal tragedies with the death of your department colleague. Believe me, that's all.'

'So, how do you think this group would help us, Xander?'

'I think it's good to talk and share. As you said with your wanting to take the Camino De Santiago trip. Sharing stories is a healing thing. It relieves the burden of feeling unique. We're not alone, Pascal.'

'I can agree on that. Not much separates us from the rest of the animal kingdom. Just that one little gene mutation past along our ancestry that makes us sentient. Which is why I got into cultural anthropology.'

'I think it will also help you stop being so hard on yourself.'

'You think I'm hard on myself?'

'I absolutely think that. You made a mistake once when you were young...and something you think you have to live with, like a wound that will never heal. But it will and you certainly don't have to live it anymore. You can let it go. It's gone. And you're not that same person, that little man-boy who didn't know who he was. You definitely know who you are now.'

He sighed. 'I suppose you're right.'

'I know I'm right. And I'm right about this Fitbit too. Come on and have a try.'

'All right, already. Jeezus, what a nag.' He laughed and kissed his partner, who kissed him back.

'We can make it work this time, Pascal. I know we can.'

'Thank you, Xander. I love you too, man.' Pascal's mobile phone buzzed just then. 'A text message from Felly,' he said, reading aloud. 'Hoi Pascal! I just wanted to let you know that Dr Huijsman approved of us working together again on another sociolinguistics project. Any thoughts? No rush. We could meet up for coffee next week. I have Wednesday open. You?'

'Ah, bless,' laughed Xander.

Felly thought it would be great working with her younger colleague again. She was worried about Pascal, but thought he was handling it all well, as well as could be expected. She sat at the kitchen countertop, perched on a barstool and drinking coffee while texting and reading the responses. The kittens were at her feet, batting the chair legs as they chased each other round, stopping and starting with comical expressions on their faces. 'What are you two nincompoops doing?' she said, laughing at them.

Femke came over just then, watching them too. 'They are poops.'

'Who's a poop?' said Kieran. He'd been out on the deck, soaking in the bit of sun their sporadic weather offered up that morning. 'Anyone up for a cycle? I feel like having friet.'

'Friet?' said Femke. 'Me, me, me. I do.'

Felly said, 'I don't feel like having bits of fried potato sitting in my belly today, but I don't mind the bike ride. Where would we go? I don't think much is open on Sunday.'

'Yer mam's place is.' He grinned showing her his phone screen. 'She just texted and asked us over. Filip and Moira are going to be there too.'

'Okay then, but we'd better bring a six-pack or two.'

'Already on it. So, get on yer hat and coat, poppie. Over the river and through the woods we go.'

The Irish have a saying that it is a bad wind that does not bring good to somebody. And no matter how bad the disclosing old secrets ended up being, Evi Anneveldt's death was a tremendous catalyst for rediscoveries and the healing of old wounds – the unsticking of what had so long been stuck – allowing all who were once involved to go on with their lives and live as well as could be expected ever after.

Betrayal of Bosch cast of characters

Felicia McNeela née van Vliet (Felly) – sociolinguist, professor at Leiden University (LU) in the Netherlands. She has recently returned to the classroom after five years of research-based studies while raising her now preschool age daughter. Felly drinks both red and white wine.

Kieran McNeela (Kier) – husband to Felly, and criminal lawyer who was recently promoted to junior partner at the De Veer Group, a Leiden law firm. When Felly met Kieran, he was an inspector with the local Irish Garda. He later followed Felly to the Netherlands and obtained a law degree at UvA, the University of Amsterdam. Paddy's is Kieran's whiskey of choice, and Murphy's Red for beer.

Femke Siobhan McNeela (Femmie, poppie) – the five-year-old daughter of Felly and Kieran, who's being raised in a trilingual household and now attending the second class of a Dutch international school in Leiden. Femke loves strawberry juice.

Pip and Puk – the mischievous household Ragdoll kittens.

Anneke van Vliet (Ankie) – Felly's blonde, hazel-eyed mother, is well into her 60s, though fit and sporty looking. Spunky and direct by nature, she teamed up with her husband early on to breed Irish Setters and is now retired. Red is Ankie's wine of choice, particularly Pinot Noir.

Martinus van Vliet (Tinus) – Felly's father, whose vibrantly turquoise eyes and chestnut hair are striking features of the otherwise tall, thin and easy-going man a few years his wife's senior. Retired with his wife from breeding Irish Setters, his current interests are in local history and museums. Tinus prefers drinking gin (Dutch Jenever).

Filip van Vliet – Felly's brother, who shares his twin sister's same colouring: the vibrant eyes and chestnut hair that was genetically inherited from their father. He's a corporate lawyer, avid surfer and a bit of a clown.

Moira van Vliet née Robinson – an Irish farmgirl whose parents once bred and showed Irish Setters alongside the van Vliets. She and Felly have been close friends over the years, and she is now married to the brother, Filip. Moira is a known kitchen diva, who is good with children though having none of her own. Her cousins, Aidan and Sean, work for the Irish coastguard in County Kerry and have stayed close to the family over the years. Her drink of choice is, well, anything.

Evi Anneveldt née van de Meervenne – an eccentric cultural anthropologist in the shared humanities department of Felly's university was also popular with her students. After finding out about her stage four lung cancer, she went home to 's-Hertogenbosch on sabbatical and had been found drowned in the Dommel River canal shortly before her university's weekend conference in a hotel only several metres away.

Pascal van Houten – the assistant professor of the cultural anthropology department, Pascal is one of the youngest of the professors at LU and keen on teaming up with Felly and their shared students in a serious gaming project. At some point in the story, Pascal rekindles his relationship with

Xander Anakotta, a young and good looking Moluccan medical coder at Erasmus Hospital.

Dean Ernst Huijsman (Dr Ernie) – the grey-eyed, shock of white hair head of the humanities department at Leiden University is an old hipster who is known for his colourful artsy looking ties, though he's not seen wearing one in this sequel. Dr Ernie still listens to Jethro Tull and encourages the varying department sections to involve themselves in cross-curriculum activities. His department secretary is the dark-eyed, chatty Jolanda Wiersman.

Dr Sebastian De Vos (Baas) – Head of the cultural anthropology department and partner to his secretary, Trudy Langmeijer.

Trudy Langmeijer – Dr De Vos's secretary who went to public school with Evi Anneveldt and makes beaded eyeglass chains as a hobby while meditating to stay calm. She is a tall, hazel-eyed woman with a helmet shaped hairdo.

Reinier Nolten – Felly and Pascal's engaging LU student, who is wearing a Grunge look. He is also the innovator of the serious game, *Whodunit: the Hounds of LU* capstone project of Felly's sociolinguistic course. He and others of his class team up with Pascal, who begins working with Felly on this shared class project.

Minke Koijma – always seen in school wearing a pinstripe jacket, she and Reinier are the programmers of the gaming project. She hooks up with Reinier as the term progresses, and they become sort of an item...sort of.

Annemiek Teakes – in lacy dress, leggings and boots, which is her preferred style, Annemiek works with fellow students, Lotte Wehkamp and Lucas Hoekstra, who are minor characters, like herself, developing the narratives for the serious gaming project.

Professor Jens Borsen – the visiting influencer from Copenhagen's Institute of Innovative Media, who is a balding man with wire-frame glasses that has been invited to the conference as its guest speaker on learning trends.

Dirk Nolten – Reinier's father, a civil engineer and entrepreneur living in Den Bosch with his wife Jenny and Reinier's younger sister, Rinske. His personal history unfolds as it entwines with the other characters throughout the story.

Bridget McNeela – Kieran's mother in County Cork, Ireland. Her husband, Captain James, passed away before Felly could meet him, leaving his wife managing well in a household of six grown children, Kieran being the fifth. The family home remains, though all but one sibling have permanently left the nest with children of their own.

Sinead Gleason née McNeela – Kieran's younger – and youngest – sister, Sinead had taught alongside Felly several summers ago in Youghal when Felly had been invited by the school to teach an adult seminar. Kieran had included Felly in a later decision to leave his home in Youghal to Sinead and her husband, Mick as a generous wedding present. At the time, this younger couple were struggling primary school teachers though now they were doing fine with a brood of their own.

Dutch police officers (politie) – Dutch officers of the law wear dark blue uniforms with yellow stripes that extend across the upper arms and chest under light bullet proof vests. The 'Politie' lettering is embossed on the left collarbone. The footwear are black lace-up boots. And blue caps with the police department logo are worn on the head with the longer haired females sporting ponytails that stick out in back of the cap.

Dutch law is generally fair-minded and balanced in its approach. Lawyers often act as counsellors, and the police are typically noncombative and seen more as friendly law enforcers in their local neighbourhoods. They can be less friendly in the bigger cities like Amsterdam; and, overall, are firm in their contact with the public when necessary.

Acknowledgements

Special thanks to Patti Bagley for her eagle-eye in the proofreading of my novel. Not only did she catch the spelling and syntactical errors I missed, but she also pointed out things and situations needing clarification to my readers. This has been particularly helpful because of my dealing with individuals from different cultures, their thoughts, words and actions all being translated into English while attempting to keep the flavour of their perspectives.

My second reader, Janet Van Bobo, deserves a big hug as a fellow expatriate living in the Netherlands even longer than I have. Her awareness of how the varying groups here meet, greet and function have been of great help to me. And, as a retired secondary school teacher, she has also been wonderful at spotting anything that hasn't set right grammatically and syntactically.

Thank you, thank you, ladies!

About the author....

Sherry Marie Gallagher's 4th book in the Felly van Vliet murder mystery series takes place in the Dutch cities of Leiden and 's-Hertogenbosch, Leiden being home to the van Vliet university professor. Felly's amateur sleuthing is done this time in the historical town of the famous 16th century painter, Jheronimus Bosch, where mystery and intrigue is brought to his masterwork: 'The Garden of Earthly Delights' while addressing its underlying themes of ethics and our choices in life.

Murder on the Rocks! is the 1st of the series, which the author wrote after a time living and working in Ireland's educational system. A special love for certain regions of its south-western counties, locals and their native dialects has prompted her, once again, to weave and spin a tale—this time a murder mystery—set in the heart of Youghal, a quaint Irish fishing village and 1950's film site of 'Moby Dick'.

Death By Chopstick, the 2nd of the series, continues the narrator's adventures during a teaching block in Beijing, China.

The Poisoned Tree, the 3rd of the series, brings the narrator's adventures full circle as she returns to teach in her own backyard, in Leiden, the Netherlands.

Boulder Blues, Ms Gallagher's first novel, is a bittersweet romance of musically talented youth from immigrant families caught up in the sex, drugs and rock'n'roll generation of America's Vietnam era.

.

Dancing Spoons and Khachapuri. During the 1998-99 economic crisis, the author experienced the harshness of an exchange professor's life while teaching a year at Moscow State University in Russia. The adventure resulted in a rich Russian tale.

Uncommon Boundaries is a compilation of shorts, poems and song written with Ms Gallagher's own students in mind. In it she sings of the beauty of living life with noted whisperings of its harsher undertones. Throughout it all, the author challenges us to experience life with grace and honesty while living it to its fullest.

Look up the website *www.aislingbooks.com* where you can have a trial read and directly purchase this and other Aisling Books.

Betrayal of Bosch—Felly van Vliet Mysteries

Lightning Source UK Ltd.
Milton Keynes UK
UKHW041649170621
385519UK00014B/111